ALSO BY AMY HEMPEL

Tumble Home

At the Gates of the Animal Kingdom

Reasons to Live

THE DOG
OF THE MARRIAGE

STORIES

Amy Hempel

SCRIBNER

New York London Toronto Sydney

SCRIBNER
1230 Avenue of the Americas
New York, NY 10020

SCRIBNER and design are trademarks of Macmillan Library Reference USA, Inc.
used under license by Simon & Schuster, the publisher of this work.

For information regarding special discounts for bulk purchases,
please contact Simon & Schuster Special Sales at
1-800-456-6798 or business@simonandschuster.com

DESIGNED BY ERICH HOBBING

Set in Garamond No. 3

Manufactured in the United States of America

1   3   5   7   9   10   8   6   4   2

Library of Congress Cataloging-in-Publication Data

Hempel, Amy.
The dog of the marriage : stories / Amy Hempel
p. cm.
Contents: Beach town—Jesus is waiting—The uninvited—Reference #388475848-5—
What were the white things?—The dog of the marriage—The afterlife—
Memoir—Offertory.
1. United States—social life and customs—Fiction. 2. Man-woman relationships—
Fiction. 3. Married people—Fiction. I. Title.
PS3558.E47916D64 2005
813'.54—dc22
2004057837

ISBN 0-7432-6451-7

FOR GORDON

But the greatest desire of all is to be
In the dream of another,
To feel a slight pull, like reins,
To feel a heavy pull, like chains.

—Yehuda Amichai

CONTENTS

THE DOG
OF THE MARRIAGE

BEACH TOWN

The house next door was rented for the summer to a couple who swore at missed croquet shots. Their music at night was loud, and I liked it; it was not music I knew. Mornings, I picked up the empties they had lobbed across the hedge, Coronas with the limes wedged inside, and pitched them back over. We had not introduced ourselves these three months.

Between our houses a tall privet hedge is backed by white pine for privacy in winter. The day I heard the voice of a woman not the wife, I went out back to a spot more heavily planted but with a break I could just see through. Now it was the man who was talking, or trying to—he started to say things he could not seem to finish. I watched the woman do something memorable to him with her mouth. Then the man pulled her up from where she had been kneeling. He said, "Maybe you're just hungry. Maybe we should get you something to eat."

The woman had a nimble laugh.

The man said, "Paris is where you and I should go."

The woman asked what was wrong with here. She said, "I like a beach town."

I wanted to phone the wife's office in the city and hear what she would sound like if she answered. I had no fellow feeling; all she had ever said to me was couldn't I mow my lawn later in the day. It was noon when she asked. I told her the village bylaws disallow mowing before seven-thirty, and that I had waited until nine. A gardener, hired by my neighbor, cared for their yard. But still I was sure they were neglecting my neighbor's orchids. All summer long I had watched for the renters to leave the house together so that I could let myself in with the key from the shelf in the shed and test the soil and water the orchids.

The woman who did not want to go to Paris said that she had to leave. "But I don't want you to leave," the man said, and she said, "Think of the kiss at the door."

Nobody thinks about the way sound carries across water. Even the water in a swimming pool. A week later, when her husband was away, the wife had friends to lunch by the pool. I didn't have to hide to listen; I was in view if they had cared to look, pulling weeds in the raspberry canes.

The women told the wife it was an opportunity for her. They said, "Fair is fair," and to do those things she might not otherwise have done. "No regrets," they said, "if you are even the type of person who is given to regret, if you even have that type of wistful temperament to begin with."

The women said, "We are not unintelligent; we just let passion prevail." They said, "Who would deny that we have all had these feelings?"

The women told the wife she would not feel this way forever. "You will feel worse, however, before you feel better, and that is just the way it always is."

The women advised long walks. They told the wife to watch the sun rise and set, to look for solace in the natural world, though they admitted there was no comfort to be found in the world and they would all be fools to expect it.

The weekend the couple next door had moved in—their rental began on Memorial Day—I heard them place a bet on the moon. She said waxing, he said waning. Days later, the moon nearly full in the night sky, I listened for the woman to tell her husband she had won, knowing they had not named the terms of the bet, and that the woman next door would collect nothing.

JESUS IS WAITING

I didn't want the sunroof or the luggage rack, but neither did I want to wait the three months not to have to have them. So I took the white one anyway and put fifty thousand miles on it in just about a year.

Lincoln Tunnel to Baltimore, BWI: two and three-quarter hours; Holland Tunnel to D.C. (Connecticut Avenue exit): three and a quarter hours. In Virginia, anything over ninety is now reckless driving and reckless driving costs more than speeding does and they say no excuses, you have to show up in court, but don't believe it; I phoned in sick the day I was slated to appear and a clerk told me where to send the check. One more reckless driving ticket in Virginia and I'll have to find the place they have the safety class that, if you take it, knocks three points off your license. Or, I don't know, your life?

Maryland and New York are the states where I can push it.

No blue highways, nothing scenic.

In a tornado outside Baltimore, in a broken neighborhood off I-95, I asked the attendant in a Mobil station, "Where's anywhere else?"

The man didn't even point.

I write in pencil because a pencil is what is tied with string to the suggestion box. "We welcome your comments." I write, "I went to the other place first, but got pissed off in line and came here and am glad I did."

I had not fared so well at the one off Exit 7. The ice machine was broken. Yes, I got more Dr Pepper in the cup, but the Dr Pepper I got was warm.

I never eat in the place I stop for gas. I like to keep the odometer turning. Sometimes I will drive only as far as a local exit with a road or avenue in the name. Not a connecting artery. I will pull off into a community, find a cul-de-sac, stop the car, keep an eye on the trees that line the street. Maybe fill out a postcard bought at a rest stop, address it to the man who won't speak to me, ask him "Is one of the symptoms that you're thirsty all the time?"

Or is one of the symptoms a rash? Is one of the symptoms dry mouth? That it's hard to urinate? Maybe one of the symptoms is that you piss people off.

Taking it more slowly since the spinout on black ice. Where were the famed antilock brakes? Traveling under the speed limit on a flat stretch of road, and all of a sudden a wreck that takes the luggage rack off. No visible injuries—you can't see a sprain—but I had to make camp for days while the sunroof was checked out. There was a multiplex and a Mexican restaurant that used baked beans in their burritos. North Carolina, but nothing Carolingian.

The guy who sold me a map in the Exxon in Greensboro asked me who I was listening to the next hundred miles. Before he had stopped speaking to me, the man back home made me a tape for the road. It's the same cut over and over on both sides—"Jesus Is Waiting," by the Reverend Al Green. Apart from those, the words you hear the most are "Thank you."

On the New Jersey Turnpike, a box of animal crackers at the Walt Whitman rest area costs almost two dollars.

Here's something I didn't know: the drag you get from open windows uses more gas than running the air conditioner does.

The radio said Dorothy Love Coates died today. But I didn't know she'd even been alive.

A point of pride not to stop when tired. Drive a couple of hundred more miles. In St. Louis, they say when you hit Indianapolis, you're home. Home is a Days Inn or a Comfort Inn, unless there is more than one of those big trucks in the lot. In the morning, in the lobby, there are free doughnuts and coffee. I like handing the sticks and the sugar and the cream around. There's always a television going so we all have a place to look. Someone will always say to me, "Have a safe trip." I'll always say, "You too."

I keep meaning to pull off and visit an IKEA store.

Before I took to the road, a friend tried to get me to go to a department store with him. He said it was to improve the place where I lived. He said, "I want to know you are reading beneath *this* lamp." This fellow was dying. He knew it and I did not. I think he was tucking me in. He was making sure all of his friends had the right lamps, the comfiest pillows, the softest sheets. He was tucking us all in for the night.

In a motel off an interstate, a breakfaster warns me about impetigo. But who in this century gets impetigo? The breakfaster says to avoid standing water. Or maybe she says standing *in* water.

Avoid it, is the point.

Listening to Al Green, I didn't mind the smell of tar, a turn lane being paved. At a farm stand along a switchback road, I bought a bag of shiny red chiles. Wouldn't they be good for whatever there was to be good for?

*　　*　　*

It is the day before Thanksgiving. According to the radio, people travel to their destinations by car. One hundred percent if you count just me.

A good feeling when I see traffic cones. They weigh next to nothing and cannot hurt a car. That's not why I mow them down.

A point of pride—to drive like crazy in the passing lane, or, alternatively, to sit in the fast lane stuck in traffic and not to register any change in heart rate or respiration. I am often moved to tears when the lane I am in merges with another. I can well up where the New Jersey Turnpike becomes 95 and where 95 becomes 85 just outside Petersburg, Virginia.

On the day before a holiday, you feel you have a destination just by being on the road with so many people who do.

Have a destination, that is.

I write on a postcard, "Is one of the symptoms a fever of unknown origin?" I sign the card, "As ever."

I put a lot of money into tires. I don't rotate—I replace, with the best new radials. I am never late for scheduled maintenance. I learned the hard way to watch that they do not dilute the windshield-wiper fluid. Except for the iffy antilock brakes, if something goes wrong, it is not the car that's at fault. Bad form to blame something for the damage one does. I just mow them down—and drive on.

Countryside: a blue-lit blue spruce in the center of a pond with swans. City: a blue neon cellular sign, pigeons pecking crumbs on the sidewalk. Did someone stand toy soldiers in wet cement? A small brigade marches around the corner.

McDonald's has better french fries and their orange juice comes in a cup that fits the holder in the car. Burger King's orange juice comes in a carton, but their fish thing is better than the one at McDonald's. I don't know about the coffee at either place. I only know about the coffee if it's in a lobby and free. I saw a forensics special on the TV at a Days Inn—it examined the mystery of three hunters who were found dead at their campsite. Extensive testing revealed that there had been a newt in their coffeepot, and when they poured in boiling water, deadly toxins were released by the newt.

Driving togs are usually black jeans and a cotton turtleneck, a wool-lined canvas jacket thrown across the front seat to put on when pumping gas. Do people still call them gas stations? Filling stations? Where are the people who call them service stations?

If I had a gas station, would I name it Exxon or Hess?

For shoes: anything that slips right off. I drive barefoot unless there's snow.

The night before Thanksgiving, I turn onto an exit ramp for the Thomas Edison rest area. In the gift shop I buy a postcard with a picture of a dog trotting down Route 66. I ask if one of the symptoms is that you can't get a song out of your head, and sign it, "More as ever than ever."

The roads on Thanksgiving Day are as quiet as they were packed the day before. Destinations must have been reached.

I can still recognize a '67 Mustang.

I was not put on this earth to fill my own tank, but I have come to look forward to doing it. I like the smell on my hands from the pump, the restrooms never not out of soap. Each time I cross a state line, I visit the Welcome Center and ask for directions. What a laugh. Then back to the car, merging confidently into traffic, seeing how far I can go before racking up "Jesus Is Waiting."

It is Thanksgiving Day. I am driving the New Jersey Turnpike. Past the exit for the store where I once bought a hat made out of a Wonder Bread wrapper. Past the exit for the house where I was talked into playing a party game called "Empty Hands." Three more exits. Past them all.

The geographic cure, these bouts of driving, with the age-old bit built in: "Wherever you go, there you are." Maybe people should be trained like dogs. But people aren't dogs. Besides, a dog won't speak to you, either.

Is one of the symptoms restlessness? An inability to stay put?

The calluses on the palms of my hands show that I have put in the hours, hit the road early and often, stayed flexible and ready to leave on short notice, on even no notice; packed in the car are clothes, bottles of juice, a pass for bridges and tunnels and tolls, assorted useless maps, and the tape he made for me—"Jesus Is Waiting."

I never stop for the night before filling the tank.

In the back is a case with the word HELP on it. It contains jumper cables, flares, a flashlight, tire patches. I should add aspirin and a knife.

God, it's an ugly road.

And now someone is following me. He's driving a black car. It trumps the pickup that pulled up alongside me in Virginia, the guy turning on his inside light so I could get a look at him. This new guy isn't bad-looking, but he has a ponytail and there is no desire in his gaze.

In a pig's eye.

Soon I'll have a chance of a bridge or tunnel. In these last years I'm talking about, I've driven a tunnel only once. Since I have a choice, when I have a choice, I choose a bridge.

In the backseat of my car, a potted amaryllis blooms.

*   *   *

Sometimes, if I were not ready to get back in the car, I would phone a realtor from my motel. I would pick a name from the phone book, and ask to be shown houses. I would give the broker a price range. I would be taken to see Colonials, a saltbox, Cape Cods. I keep the business cards in a pocket of the case labeled HELP.

The drive is determinedly a drive. Mostly it is just about the sounds of the car, of driving, of the fade-in and fade-out of the radio, the removal from everything but the moving body in a vehicle, of the is-ness of passing from here to there, of not being where you were, of Jesus waiting. Call it a meditation. Call it *drone*. How else to approach Jesus than without history, without reason, without restraint? And buoyed by staying in motion away from everything, the mind become the traveling until wherever you stop, won't Jesus be waiting there?

Is one of the symptoms a loss of faith? Or faith in loss?

On the way back into the city, I stop to fill up. I would like to be scrambled and served with sausages at an all-night diner.

Is this what the world is?

I smell my fingers. Nice.

This time I use the telephone instead of sending a card. I leave him a message. I say I will be there in an hour. I say, "Can we take each other in?"

Back in the car I adjust the seat so I will have to sit up straighter. I take a mint from the glove compartment and twist off the wrapper.

I see myself in the rearview mirror.

I give the car some gas, and merge with the other drivers who are heading into the city where Jesus is waiting—or isn't.

THE UNINVITED

It was one and two and three and four and five o'clock in the morning. Whatever time it was, it was time to take the test. You did not have to wait until morning anymore; the instructions on the box said that for an accurate result you could dip the strip of litmus paper in a "clear stream of urine" any time of day. My waiting until morning was habit, a nod to the old days when "first morning's urine" was going to give you the answer. Though not at home. You had to go to a clinic then. Sometimes on the ceilings of exam rooms was a sign: "A woman can never be too thin or too rich, or too close to the end of the table."

I was fifty years old, and ten days late.

If menopausal, go on estrogen; if pregnant, go on welfare.

If I *was* pregnant, I did not know who to blame— my husband, whom I did not live with, or the man in the auditorium, whom I did not report.

I did what I had always done the night before taking the test: I watched *The Uninvited.*

"The cold . . . is no mere matter of degrees Fahrenheit, but a drawing of warmth from the vital centers of the living."

The Uninvited, made in 1944, stars Ray Milland and Ruth Hussey as the English brother and sister Roderick and Pamela Fitzgerald, who happen upon a stately empty house on a cliff in Cornwall when they are on vacation. The two are so won over by the place they decide to buy it and leave their London lives—he a composer and music critic, she a budding homemaker—for these "haunted shores."

"That's not because there are *more* ghosts here than in other places, mind you, it's just that the people who live hereabouts are more . . ."

I am courting ghosts at a place where ghosts are studied as a subset of the paranormal. I participate in experiments at an institute in the South. Last week I was placed in a private room and given a photograph to hold. I was supposed to try to "send" the image to a woman in another room down the hall. The photograph I held was a likeness of Frankenstein, a still from the movie. For nearly half an hour I stared and directed the thought: *Frankenstein, Frankenstein,* at the woman down the hall. A researcher came to get us and took us downstairs to appear before the staff.

"Well?" the researcher prompted.

The woman from down the hall said, "I don't know, I kept getting Frank, Frank—*Frank Sinatra?*"

And I screamed, "That's a match!"—wanting so much the unexplainable in my life.

I had not been living in my house for months. I had accepted a job house-sitting, if you can call that a job, for a professor on sabbatical from a university in the South. He had hired a cleaning lady and a gardener, so all I had to do was occupy space and forward his mail. He would return for spring break, at which time I was to return to my house up North. Since it was winter up there, I returned for a night every three or four weeks; I had to check for burst pipes and whatever else could happen in my absence.

When I was back home, I read the local newspaper's weekly police blotter. It featured the usual thefts—houses closed for the winter are routinely broken into—as well as a range of conceptual crimes. Someone had turned up the thermostat in a beach house in the dunes. This person took nothing, but turned the temperature to ninety degrees, which, by the time it was discovered, had badly warped the floors. In another house, the owners discovered that someone had emptied the kitchen cabinets. Nothing had been stolen, but every item in the cabinets had been lined up neatly on the counters.

One kind of damage presented itself on my first visit home: the house smelled of mice, and when I lay still on the couch, I heard them scrabbling in the cabinets and behind the walls. There was no point setting out traps— I would be leaving the next day and anything caught would decompose in the weeks until my next visit. I could hear mice in a drawer. I yanked it open and found droppings like fat, dark grains of rice surrounding a diamond-and-sapphire pin my mother-in-law had given me when I married her son. When the marriage ended, I thought of giving the pin back to my husband; his parents had since died, and the pin had been a gift to his mother from his father. I thought about it, but I did nothing about it, and now the timeworn jewelry was in this sorry setting when it should have been safe in a tiny velvet pouch.

All of us should be safe in a tiny velvet pouch.

Well, I left the thing loose in the drawer.

And of course a pipe did burst, but luckily one outside, positioned to irrigate a cutting garden long since abandoned, the garden my husband's project, so I kept the water turned off except to flush a toilet when I would turn the relevant lever in the basement, go back upstairs and flush, then turn off the water again. Think of it as fancy camping, I told myself, and it was fine, this manner of thinking.

For instance, storm doors and windows had never been put up, so, like clocks not changed from Daylight Savings Time, wouldn't the absence of these fixtures be just right in a few more months?

Lightbulbs, that was a different matter. They were often burned out, however much they had not been used. So I just as often had to stand on one foot to change them in the kitchen.

"Important decisions have to be made quickly," says Pamela Fitzgerald.

"Anyway, how do you even know it's for sale?" says brother Roderick.

"Life isn't as cruel as that—it's *got* to be," says Pamela Fitzgerald.

Important decisions do have to be made quickly. Once the test stick is removed from its foil packet, once the "absorbent tip" is placed in the urine flow for at least five seconds, or dipped into a clean container of this person's urine, also for no fewer than five seconds, the result will be indicated in three minutes.

A decision will be made quickly, and not at all quickly forgotten.

There is a "sealed splashguard" on the test stick. Still, it seems smarter to collect the urine and place the test stick in the container. So the first decision of the morning is whether to go in a tumbler or a measuring cup. In crystal or in cookware?

At the video store in the town in the South, I rent *Topper* and *The Ghost and Mrs. Muir*—romantic, playful, companionable ghosts—but they don't compare with the ghost who sobs all night on the estate of Windward

House where, from a cliff, young Mary Meredith falls (or is pushed?) to her death.

The night before taking the test the first time I had to take it, I watched *The Uninvited* on television, on the all-night oldies channel. I took it as a sign, its broadcast that night. The next morning, every minute of which I watched approach, I tested positive. It was a spring day in Southern California. It was 1970, and I was in college.

One week later, I signed a statement that would be sent to a committee of physicians. In it, I threatened to take my life if I were not allowed to terminate the pregnancy. A woman I barely knew had coached me to say this; she was the wife of a friend of a friend and had been moved to help a young thing she barely knew because she had been the young thing's age and it had not been easy for her. Or so I seemed to have thought.

I was a girl again.

I stood in the student union, studying the bulletin board.

What could have been better proof of girlhood re-acquired?

It is the little terrier, Bobby, who first gets Pamela and Rick into Windward House. Bobby sets off across the lawn after a squirrel and squeezes in after it when the squirrel slips through an open window. Bobby chases the squirrel up the chimney, but refuses to mount the stairs, where his owners will find, behind the locked door of the studio, an unexplained chill and a despair that engulfs all who enter.

My own house is situated across the street from a cemetery. The lawn of "the Boneyard," as I call the place, is littered with dozens of chewed-out marrow bones. Neighbors would complain if the privet did not thrive and block the yard from view. The bones come frozen in packages of six; neighbor dogs get one apiece when they stop by to visit. They follow me across the lawn, back behind the backyard to where the growth has been too much to keep up with. The cold frame where seedlings made a dash for it is filled with weeds, and the rows of sunflowers and gladioli and irises are lost under grasses so long they bend and swirl into bedding for deer. The grasses have buried the rows of strawberries that my husband protected with net until the morning I went to pick some to serve with cream and found a box turtle caught in the webbing, dead. Like the "ghost nets" left behind by fishermen, seines that float loose to entangle porpoises and diving gulls.

That day I ripped off the net.

Let everything eat.

I did not call the police. Two years of working a hotline, and I did not report it.

We always offered to accompany victims to court.

We offered follow-up support until a woman called to say she was moving and could a few of us come over and help her pack.

Some of the group never said the word *man*. Instead they said "potential rapist." There were men who wanted to donate money, but there was a faction among us who did not feel right accepting donations from future rapists.

Here is what I would have had to say, if I had been a caller: "Hello? Hello? Oh, man, I did not call the police because I had invited the man in. My clothes? I took them off myself."

The time I tried to keep it, I did not try for very long. Although one week did seem to me like a long time. I was sick enough to be in a hospital with an intravenous drip plugged into my wrist. There was an antiemetic I could ask for twice a day that made life tolerable for a little less than half an hour. Sometimes the body takes over to make a decision the mind can't make. This was one of the doctors. She said sometimes a woman thinks she wants a child when what she really wants is the father of the child.

Stella Meredith was only three years old when her mother died at Windward House. Now twenty, she lives with her grandfather, the Commander (Donald Crisp), in town. Stella, played by Gail Russell, meets the Fitzgeralds when they come to inquire about buying the deserted house on the cliff. Stella is rude to them, tells them the house is not for sale. But her grandfather arrives as she is ushering them out, and, keen to provide for Stella after he is gone, sells the Fitzgeralds the house on the spot. The grandfather does not mention the disturbances the new owners will find. Stella, meanwhile, has caught Roderick Fitzgerald's eye; later, he will readily accept her apology and invite Stella to dinner at her former home.

The act of taking the test made me feel sick. Before I could insert the test strip into the glass, I had to lie down and wait for the room to get steady. I wanted the hospital staple, Jell-O, cubed in a bowl on a tray. At home—a different story; was the problem sliced bananas or canned pears? The weight of diced peaches, the pits in the cherries? Waterlogged chunks of pineapple, fan-shaped mandarin oranges; they sank to the bottom or they rested on the surface—you had to know more about Jell-O than I did.

Mrs. Wynn used to make me Jell-O. She was a frequent baby-sitter, and, apart from my acquaintances in the movies, the only English person I knew. She was inventive, and once pasted the feet of paper dolls to either side of a Mexican jumping bean. She attached tissue skirts that covered the beans and then placed the dolls on a plate set on top of a chafing dish. In due course, the "fairies" had all been made to dance.

When I was sick, Mrs. Wynn performed a trick she called "the Passenger to Boulogne." She brought to my bedroom an orange and a wineglass and a penknife and handkerchief. She prepared the orange by cutting into the rind the best ears, nose, and mouth her skill could devise. She then smoothed out the handkerchief and stretched it lightly over the mouth of the wineglass; she set the carved orange thereon. When she saw that she had my attention, she moved the handkerchief backward and forward over the top of the glass, imparting to the orange a rolling motion and what she described to her woozy audience as the agonies of a seasick passenger making the Channel crossing. The performance, she explained, was supposed to end by draping the handkerchief like a hood over the "head" and squeezing the orange into the glass. In deference to my condition, however, Mrs. Wynn demurred, saying some people found it disagreeably realistic.

I thought I remembered a Mrs. Wynn from *The Uninvited,* but the devoted housekeeper the Fitzgeralds bring over from London is named Lizzie Flynn, not Wynn. She hectors and pampers Pamela and Rick; she makes them tipsy pudding. A superstitious woman, Lizzie Flynn is not long for Windward House. Soon she is spending nights in a farmhouse down the road where, presumably, no ghost can be heard sobbing until dawn.

On the hotline one night, I got a call from a local rock star. The woman was calling between sets to say that the man who had attacked her the week before was sitting in the audience.

Had she reported that attack the week before? No, she said, she had had a few drinks that night. Did she want me to call the police? No, but could I meet her at the club after the show?

We always went out in pairs, so I called another counselor, a resourceful dyke named Carolee. The bouncer waved us in. We stood in the back and watched the end of the show. The rocker was athletic, backlit, barely clothed. Carolee and I worked our way to the greenroom as the rocker came off the stage. I tapped my chest, and she came over and hugged me hard. With her arm around me, she walked me to where I could see the audience from behind a curtain. She pointed to a man alone.

"There's my rapist," she said.

Then, as was not uncommon, she wanted to know if she had put us to any trouble. I reminded her that I was already on call, and Carolee said she preferred this to the fight she had been having with her girlfriend. Lesbian fights are the worst, Carolee said—nobody ever walks out and slams the door because they're both women and want to talk about their *feelings*.

On the drive back home from the house-sitting job, I stopped off in West Virginia to meet my estranged husband. The large house sat on three hundred acres of horse and dairy farm amid gentle hills cut through by the

Opequon Creek. His family staged fraught reunions every summer and lobbied for repairs needed to keep the place up. There were thirteen bedrooms and one bathroom, added in the 1920s. Each summer we all scraped and repainted the wraparound porch, taking breaks to chase off trespassers who pushed metal detectors across the grounds. My first time there, a charter bus wound up the drive on a hot afternoon. It advertised "The J.E.B. Stuart Singers," who dismounted—a busload of folks in period costume. They serenaded us with Civil War ballads. My husband—then-husband—allowed as how the family was used to this.

Over the years, the affable and ineffectual caretaker would phone to report break-ins and thefts. The great house was vacant except for reunions, encouraging thieves to back their trucks up to the wide front doors. They stole every piece of furniture. They were so unhurried as to remove and leave behind cheap replacement shades for the valuable antique lamps. Some of the thieves took time for a beer, and left crushed cans in the grand entry hall. By the time the family voted funds for an alarm, there was nothing of value left to protect.

The place had its ghost, of course. It was said she haunted the third floor, a well-defined apparition wearing a long white sleeping gown. I was told that the only people who saw this ghost ("the White Lady") were women who married into the family and of whom the White Lady approved. So one night I faked a rattled look and told my future husband that I had just seen a ghost when I went upstairs for more pillows. Years later, I asked this same man, now an ex-husband, if I could stay in his house to break up the long drive north and let some bad weather pass.

Was there a ghost who appeared to women *leaving* the family?

For extra class credit, we could volunteer for experiments at the parapsychology institute. These experiments took place on Saturday mornings. Downstairs, in the white clapboard house where the experiments were conducted, was a comfortable living room and library with worn, overstuffed chairs and dozens of psi journals. Across the hall was a dining room turned conference room with a rolling blackboard facing the large oval table. The research assistants were in their late twenties, conservatively dressed and courteous. My first time there, I was told to remain seated in the living room while an assistant went upstairs and turned on a computer. A photograph would appear on the screen. I was to concentrate on the image for a time, and draw it as best I could on the sheet of paper she gave me. All the assistant would say about the photograph was that there were no human beings in it.

I did as I was told.

I was about to begin sketching a cliff-dweller village

along the lines of Mesa Verde when a more powerful image took its place. I roughed in the sides of a cliff, but instead of a village I drew a Niagara Falls–like waterfall.

Upstairs, the research assistant showed me the computer screen. It displayed a wide-angle view of the Vatican in Rome. We laughed it off, and she said it was only my first try. She said why didn't we take a peek at what the next volunteer would try to draw. She pressed a button, and my waterfall appeared onscreen.

"See?" she said, pleased. "I've seen this happen before."

She turned off the light in the room.

The grand chandeliers of Windward House supplement the light on the ceilings that is reflected off the water at the base of the cliffs.

Home on spring break, when I was already five days late, I went through closets and drawers to give my things away. Was this the beginning of the famed nesting instinct? Or its opposite? A friend had once opened a drawer in his kitchen and found four banana peels neatly folded by his pregnant wife. During the winter, mice carried cereal into the fingers of my gloves.

When I was six days late, I tried to fix the soaker hose ruined months before by a power mower. It fed a long stretch of privet. I found a length of replacement hose in the unlocked garage and battled it into place for more than an hour. When I turned on the water, I saw that the hose was a regular rubber hose without the tiny perforations of the soaker. I went inside the house and got a steak knife from the kitchen. I took it outdoors and stabbed the twenty-five feet of rubber repeatedly, making my own goddamn soaker hose.

Just when you begin to think you've dreamt it, it comes again. This is Pamela Fitzgerald, talking to her brother about the ghost who sobs all night in Windward House.

Back in Los Angeles, when the woman I barely knew drove me to the hospital, we listened to somebody talking about old movies. But the movies being talked about, not one of them was as old as *The Uninvited.*

There was no blaming a poltergeist for the vase that flew off the mantel and shattered on the slate below. You had only to see that it was filled with top-heavy gerbera daisies to predict that the slightest stirring of the air, as from a person walking past, could cause the vase to topple over. As I sponged up the water and swept up the broken glass, I thought, What a relief, this loss.

The vase broke when I was seven days late. On the eighth day, I went to a lecture by a woman known as much for her compassion as for her clear soprano voice. She spoke of her work with the dying. She would bring her harp to their bedsides and sing.

"This is not ambient goodwill, not a bedside concert," she said. "It is palliative, prescriptive music. The harp invites the listener into the present so that something new can happen. Ideally, the music will make time stop—it will help unbind the dying from qualities of time that we are bound to."

She said she never sang the songs that people knew because to do so would be to hold the dying when the point is to help the dying let go. Chances are they have not heard "Rosa Mystica," or "Custodes Hominum," or "Dans Nos Obscurites," she said.

I asked her privately, when she had finished speaking, how the medical profession had first greeted her approach to the dying. She said she was invited to keep it to herself. She smiled and said, "Containment is also holy," a woman who could bide her time.

I had always thought women's clinics should replace their posters of "The Desiderata" and Erté's Nouveau nymphs with reproductions of Hans Holbein's *An Allegory of Passion,* with its caption from Petrarch's *Canzoniere*: *"E cosi desio me mena"*—"And so desire carries me along."

It is not always a matter of being careless, you know.

It is not always desire, either. Except as the desire to save oneself by doing what one is told to do by the person who has the knife.

*   *   *

An old friend from high school phoned on the ninth day I was late. She was in my town for the day. A tiny blond girl, she had left school for Japan where she put on ceremonial robes and apprenticed herself to elderly Japanese masters of the bamboo flute called *shakuhachi*. She was a quick study, and was soon quite the thing in performances throughout Japan. Back in this country, she told me she was recording "telepathic duets" with a partner on recorder two thousand miles away. She said that at an agreed-upon time, they would sit in meditation for an hour, then record an improvisation in their separate studios. Later, they would combine the two recordings into one piece.

Successful collaborations inspire envy in me. But "collaborate," someone once told me, also means "to betray."

I drove my crazy old friend to the train station that evening, and on the way home stopped at the all-night drugstore to buy the test.

When Stella first visits Windward House for dinner, a malevolent spirit causes her to faint. Pamela Fitzgerald calls for the doctor, who proves to be handsome, kind, and available. But will Pamela Fitzgerald be excluded from the happiness her brother and Stella share?

*   *   *

Crime around here has taken a new turn. People who live on the horse farms on the road to the beach report that the rails are disappearing from their split-rail fences. Charred rails are found in the sand. Imagine the kind of person who takes down someone's fence in order to make a bonfire on a beach.

Even when it was not my fault, I was lectured on the imperative of responsibility, a sitting dog being told to sit.

In the bathroom, I lifted the test strip out of the crystal tumbler. Without looking at it, I laid it on a saucer and left the room.

The next day, I took the train to the South to resume my house-sitting job. With time to kill in Union Station, I visited stores I would not otherwise have entered and underwent a kind of awakening, asking myself for the first time, Why don't I have shoe trees? Though I hadn't asked for help, a salesgirl at a cosmetics counter told me to comb my hair out wet. She said brushing stretched the hair, snapped it off. She sold me a comb, and I acted as though I had always known to use one.

You can do anything with ease if you act as though

you do it all the time—dance, sunbathe nude, talk someone out of hurting you. What had prepared me to be
good at that? I read in a psi journal that a superficially
injured person often becomes hysterical, while someone
hurt seriously may be more likely to conserve energy
and get herself help.

The evening the man in the auditorium came to my
place, I became steadily calmer until I was in a trance of
self-preservation. I had missed a lecture just before we
were to have an exam. The man to my right, always to my
right, told me he had taken thorough notes; he said he
was willing to share them with me if I wanted. He made
a show of looking in his book bag. He looked again and
said he must have left his notebook at home. He said he
could drop it off for me that evening. He said it would be
no trouble. I gave him my address, which he wrote on his
hand with a felt-tipped marker.

Well, he had the book bag with him when he showed
up at my place that night. I saw that he had changed from
a T-shirt to something long-sleeved. He came in after
standing out there for so long I felt I had to let him. He
said he just wanted to drop off the notes. He sat in the
armchair in the small living room furnished by the professor and his wife. There were no photographs of them,
but there were, I remember, a lot of wood carvings from
various foreign places. He dropped his book bag on the

carpet beside him, but did not open it. I went to get him some soda or something. Was it just water?

In the crisis training I received in the women's group, we were told that our instincts were good, that if we sensed we were being followed, we were probably right.

I said, "How about the notes?"

He looked startled, then said, with exaggerated deference, "Of course. Don't let me keep the lady waiting."

He unbuckled the book bag.

I went to switch on a lamp.

When I turned around, he had the knife.

On the hotline one night, I took a call from a woman who had been raped by three men in a Turkish bath. "Why me?" she kept asking me. I told her it happens to anyone. I told her the stats for our city. I told her it was not her fault. Then it was revealed that she weighed nearly three hundred pounds, and that what she meant by "Why me?" was why they would want to rape *her*.

"What are you doing?" I said.

He had a close-trimmed black beard, I noticed. I have never understood how a man trims a beard. Is it the lawnmower principle, where you raise the blade away from what you are going to mow?

He said, "You have a great mouth."

I said thank you.

He said he liked it that I was cordial. He said he didn't like it when a woman tried to run away, or push him away, and he had to use the knife.

Just when you begin to think you've dreamt it . . .

He tried and tried.

Said it was my fault.

I heard a dog bark outside. I didn't know the neighbors, but I knew their dog. He sometimes followed me into the house where I kept a box of biscuits for him.

"Stay," I said to the man from the auditorium.

He stopped slamming himself against me.

"It's enough that you're here," I said.

I saw his shoulders drop. He put the knife down. He put his arms around me. He said we would be lovers. He began to cry. I felt him begin to get hard.

The moment when Stella is saved from death on the cliffs is the moment the ghost stops sobbing, the moment Stella finds out who her real mother is, and what happened to her real mother when Stella was too young to know.

*   *   *

In spring, daffodils line the miles of the National Trust coastline of Cornwall. They flourish in my sorry northern yard, as well, passed over by deer as are the garish forsythia I failed to prune. It is the opposite of *ikebana,* the harmonious placement of a single bloom, and that is as close as I have ever come to making friends with disorder.

Given the number of times I have seen *The Uninvited,* you would think I would know to whom the title refers—to the ghosts or to the guests.

One of the assistants let me in when I arrived. Several handlers were already present, one for each of the dogs that would participate in the experiment.

The assistant signaled for a black Lab to be brought forward. The dog stood calmly. The assistant took a metal choke chain from her pocket. She moved to the dog's rear end. She stood above the dog and held the chain collar from one end so that it hung a few inches above the dog's hips.

"Keep her still?" the assistant said.

In a few moments, the chain began to move slowly from side to side, about an inch in each direction over the dog's hips.

"It's not scientific," said the assistant, "but it's about a hundred percent accurate in determining pregnancy.

She'll have her sonogram to be sure, but if she wasn't pregnant, the chain would have swung north-south. Something to do with the magnetic field."

The assistant handed me the chain and said, "Would you like to try it?"

I said I would.

I gave her back the chain.

I got down on all fours.

REFERENCE #388475848-5

To: Parking Violations Bureau, New York City

I am writing in reference to the ticket I was issued today for "covering 'The Empire State' " on my license plate. I include two photographs I took this afternoon that show, front and back, that the words "The Empire State" *are* clearly visible. I noticed several cars on the same block featuring license plates on which these words were entirely covered by the frame provided by the car dealer, and I noticed that none of these cars had been ticketed, as mine had. I don't mean to appear insolent, but I am wondering if the ticket might have been issued by the young Hispanic guy I sometimes see patrolling the double-parked cars during the week? I ask because the other day my dog yanked the leash from my hand and ran to him and jumped up looking for a treat. He did not appear to be comfortable around dogs, and though mine is a friendly one, she's big, and maybe the guy was frightened for a moment? It happened as I was getting out of my car, so he would have known it was *my* car, is what I'm saying.

"The Empire State"—it occurred to me that this is a nickname. I mean, police officers do not put out an all-points bulletin in The Empire State, they put out an all-points bulletin in *New York,* which words are also clearly visible on my license plates. In fact, there is no information the government might require that is not visible on these plates. You could even say that the words "The Empire State" are *advertising.* They fit a standard definition: a paid announcement, a public notice in print to induce people to use something, the action of making that thing generally known, providing information of general interest. Close enough.

I have parked my car with the plates as they appear in the accompanying photos on New York City streets for five years, since I drove the car out of the dealership on the Island five years ago; it has never been a problem until now. (I bought the car without ever reading *Consumer Reports.* I checked with a friend who said the price I was quoted was a reasonable one, but that I should refuse the extended warranty the dealer was pushing. "I'm trying to do you a favor," the dealer said, pissed off.)

At the time I bought the car, I didn't know I would soon be back living in the city, and hardly ever needing it. I had thought I would stay the two-hour drive east. What is the saying?—"If you want to make God laugh, tell him your plans."

I haven't kept track of everything I'm supposed to do with the car, but your records will show that I paid the ticket for my expired registration the same week it was issued. I did better with the safety inspection, and FYI, I'm good through November.

It's not really about the money, the $75 the ticket would cost me. I wouldn't mind writing a check for that amount as a donation to a Police Athletic League, or a fund to help rebuild the city. I'm not like the guy at the film festival yesterday who asked the French director in the Q and A after his film was shown, "Are we going to get our money back?" I hadn't even wanted to see the film; before we went, I told my date what I did want to see, and he said, "They stole the idea from that other one, the one where they ate each other." And I said, "No, that was the plane crash; this is the two guys who had the mountain-climbing accident. It's a documentary." And he said, "What isn't?"

Then, after the French film, after the audience applauded for this *major piece of crap,* the date and I cut out and went to a place he had heard about in the East Village for tea. It turned out to be someone's exotic version of high tea, so instead of scones and clotted cream and cucumber sandwiches, we were each served a teaspoon of clear, rosemary-scented jelly with a single pomegranate seed inside! What came after that were these teensy cubes of polenta covered in grapefruit puree, all floating in a "bubble bath" of champagne. Then came a chocolate truffle the size of a tooth. The fellow and I were giddy. It was pouring outside, and when we left, after the tea ceremony, we didn't want to leave each other, so we walked another couple of blocks to see a second movie, one he wanted to see, and I didn't tell him I had already seen it because by that time I just wanted to sit next to him in the dark. "I wonder who that is singing," I whispered at one point in the sound track. He didn't know, but I did, from having read the credits the first time I saw the movie. "Kind of sounds like Dave Matthews," I said, knowing I was right. "Let's be sure to check at the end," I said. "I'd like to get it for you."

Music keeps you youthful. Like I'm not the target audience for the Verve, but this morning I put on that song that goes, "I'm a million different people from one day to the next—I can change, I can change . . ." and—what's my point? I was in a really good mood when I found the ticket on my windshield. Then how to get rid of the poison, like adrenaline, that flooded my system when I read what it was for?

There is a theory of healing based on animals in the wild. People have observed animals that barely escaped a predator, and they say these animals lie down and *shake,* and in so doing somehow release the trauma. Whereas human beings take it in; we don't work it out, so it lodges in us where it produces any number of nasty effects and symptoms. If you follow a kind of guided fantasy, supposedly you can locate a calm, still place inside you and practice visiting it over and over, and that's as far as I got with this theory. It's supposed to make you feel better.

Maybe I should sell the car. But there is something about being able to get in a car and *leave* when you want to, or need to, without waiting to get to a car rental agency if you even know where one is and if it is even open when you get there.

Like last week, after a guy grabbed my arm when I was running around the reservoir, when he was suddenly in front of me, coming from the trees on the south end of the track, and no one else was around just then and I couldn't swing around wide enough to get completely past him, and he grabbed my arm. I think it was my anger that made him finally release me, because that is what I felt, not fear, until I got back home with a sore throat from yelling at him to leave me the fuck alone. I was shaking like crazy, and it wouldn't stop, so I walked a block to where my car was parked, and I drove for a couple of hours toward the ocean. My right leg was bouncing on the accelerator from nerves for much of the way, but I stopped for coffee and when I started up again I steered with my knees, the way *real* drivers steer, with a cup of coffee in one hand, playing the radio with the other. So maybe I am a wild animal, shaking off the trauma of near-capture.

There were actually two men at the reservoir. And I thought it was odd that when the first one grabbed me, and I reflexively swung my free arm around to sock him in the chest, the other man didn't stop me. Because he could have. He watched, and listened to me yell, so I don't know what the deal was. But I think it was worth paying the insurance and having to park the car and get this ticket to have the car there to use that day.

You could accuse me of trying to put a human face on this. And you would be correct. But is there anything wrong with that? Unless the ticket was issued by the guy my dog startled, I know it isn't personal. But I'm not a person who can take this ticket in stride with the kind of urbanity urbane people prize in each other. I feel I must question—and protest—this particular ticket.

I want what is fair. I don't want a fight. But the truth is, I'm shaking—right now, writing this letter. My hand is shaking while I write. It's saying what I can't say— this is the way I say it.

WHAT WERE
THE WHITE THINGS?

These pieces of crockery are a repertory company, playing roles in each dream. No, that's not the way it started. He said the pieces of crockery played roles in each *painting*. The artist clicked through slides of still lifes he had painted over thirty years. Someone in the small, attentive audience said, "Isn't that the cup in the painting from years ago?" Yes, it was, the artist said, and the pitcher and mixing bowl and goblet, too. Who was the nude woman leaning against the table on which the crockery was displayed? The artist didn't say, and no one in the small, attentive audience asked.

I was content to look at objects that had held the attention of a gifted man for so many years. I arrived at the lecture on my way to someplace else, an appointment with a doctor my doctor had arranged. Two days before, she was telling me his name and address and I have to say, I stopped listening, even though—or because—it was important. So instead of going to the radiologist's office,

I walked into a nondenominational church where the artist's presentation was advertised on a plaque outside: "Finding the Mystery in Clarity." Was this not the opposite of what most people sought? I thought, I will learn something!

The crockery was white, not glazed, and painted realistically. The pieces threw different lengths of shadows depending on the angle of the light in each painting. Sometimes the pieces were lined up touching one another, and other times there were gaps. Were these gaps part of the mystery the artist had in mind? Did he mean for us to be literal, to think: absence? He said the mind wants to make sense of a thing, the mind wants to know what something stands for. Okay, the artist said, here is what I painted that September. On the screen, we saw a familiar tabletop—familiar from years of his still lifes—and the two tallest pieces of crockery, the pitcher and the vase, were missing; nothing stood in their places.

Ahhhh, the small, attentive audience said.

Then someone asked the artist, What were the white things? He meant what were the white things in the other paintings. What did they represent? And the artist said that was not a question he would answer.

My mother, near the end of her life, announced that she was giving everything away. She was enraged. She told me to put a sticker on anything I wanted to keep, but every time I did, she said she had promised the thing to someone else. The house was all the houses I had grown up in. The things I wanted to keep were all white. But what *were* the white things?

After the lecture, I tried to remember what I had wanted to keep. But all I could say was that the things I wanted to keep were white.

After the lecture, a call to my doctor's receptionist, and I had the address of the specialist. I wasn't so late that he wouldn't see me.

When the films were developed, an assistant brought them into the examination room. The doctor placed them up against lights and pointed out the distinct spots he said my doctor had suspected he would find. I told him I would have thought the spots would be dark. I said, Is this not what most people would expect?

The doctor told me the meaning of what we looked at on the film. He asked me if I understood what he said. I said yes. I said yes, and that I wanted to ask one question: What were the white things?

The doctor said he would explain it to me again, and proceeded to tell me a second time. He asked me if this time I understood what he had told me. Yes, I said. I said, Yes, but what were the white things?

THE DOG OF THE MARRIAGE

1.

On the last night of the marriage, my husband and I went to the ballet. We sat behind a blind man; his guide dog, in harness, lay beside him in the aisle of the theater. I could not keep my attention on the performance; instead, I watched the guide dog watch the performance. Throughout the evening, the dog's head moved, following the dancers across the stage. Every so often the dog would whimper slightly. "Because he can hear high notes we can't?" my husband said. "No," I said, "because he was disappointed in the choreography."

I work with these dogs every day, and their capability, their decency, shames me.

I am trying not to take things personally. This on advice from the evaluator at the school for the blind where I train dogs. She had overheard me ask a Labrador retriever, "Are you *trying* to ruin my day?"

I suppose there are many things one should try not to take personally. An absence of convenient parking, inclement weather, a husband who finds that he loves someone else.

When I get low, I take a retired guide dog to the local hospital. Any time is good, but around the holidays is best. I will dress a handsome shepherd in a Santa suit and visit the Catholic hospital and bust in on the morning spiritual counseling. Once I heard a nun ask a patient if he was nervous about the test that was scheduled for him that afternoon, and the patient, a young man, told the nun he hadn't known there *was* a test scheduled, but now that he did, he could truthfully say that, yes, he was nervous. Then he saw "Santa" in the hallway outside his door and called, "My God! Get that dog in here!" And so we perform a service.

At work, what I technically do is *pre*-train. I do basic obedience and then some. If I am successful, and the dog has the desired temperament, a more skilled trainer will work for months to turn the dog into a guide for a blind partner. I don't know any blind people. I'm in it for the dogs. Although I remember the job interview I had before this job. I thought I might like to work in the music business, but my husband urged me in the direction of my first love: dogs. The man who would have been my employer at the record company asked me why I wanted to work there. I said, "Because I love music," and he said, "Maybe the love affair is best carried on outside the office."

"Are guide dogs happy?" my husband asked at the start. I considered this, and cited the expert who believes that an animal's happiness derives from doing his job. So in that respect, yes, I said, I would think that guide dogs are happy. "Then why do they all look like Eleanor Roosevelt?" he said.

I told him about the way they get to know you. Not the way people do, the way people flatter you by wanting to know every last thing about you, only it isn't a compliment, it is just efficient, a person getting more quickly to the end of you. Correction—dogs *do* want to know every last thing about you. They take in the smell of you, they know from the next room, asleep, when a mood settles over you. The difference is there's not an end to it.

I could tell my husband now about Goodman in the garden. I raised Goodman myself—solid black Lab—and, after a year, I gave him up, the way you do, for further training and a life with Alice Banks. Alice was a gardener. She and her husband relaxed on weekends tending beds of annuals and several kinds of tomatoes. When Alice and Goodman graduated from the program, Alice said I was welcome to stay in touch. It is always the blind person's call. We exchanged letters for several months, and in the spring, I sent her a package of things for the yard. Then I got a letter from Alice's husband, Paul. He said they had been weeding in the garden, Goodman off-duty and retrieving a tossed ball. When Goodman found himself in the tomato patch, Paul wrote, he picked something up in his mouth and began yipping with excitement, tossing the thing into the air and running in circles to retrieve it. Paul told me that Goodman had found one of the sachets I had made to keep away deer; it was a packet of cheesecloth stuffed with my hair.

That is how I like to be known.

It was something I learned from my husband, who trusted natural ways to keep predators away.

Today I am known as the Unusual Person. This is a test wherein I pull my windbreaker up over my head from behind and stagger around the corner and lurch menacingly down the walkway toward the dog-in-training. A volunteer will have the dog on a lead and attempt to walk the dog past me. We will see if the dog startles or balks or demonstrates curiosity; if the dog does startle, we'll see if he recovers quickly and continues on his way.

Before lunch I test half a dozen dogs. The first one walks by without more than a glance—he is being raised in New York City. The suburban dogs are skittish when they pass, but only one barks, and on the second approach, she, too, is quiet and passes. I am not a threat.

I eat quickly and head over across the quad to the best part of this place, the Whelping Center. The broods are brought here a couple of days before their due dates and are settled in quiet kennels where there will be a quilt on the floor and a handful of biscuits waiting. Chicken soup for dinner. The women who work here are unflappable and funny and intuitive and have substantial personalities, though they are, some of them, elfin—if only *I* had been raised here, is what I'm saying.

I contrive excuses to bring myself often to the Whelping Center. Sometimes I scoot into a kennel and warm my hands under the heat lamp trained over the newborns sleeping inside a plastic kiddie pool lined with towels, their eyes not yet open, their ears leathery tabs. I feel, here, optimistic, yet hopeful. Jubilant, yet happy. This is the way I thought and spoke for an irritating year as a girl, annoying the teachers at the girls' school I attended. In school I was diligent, yet hardworking. The headmistress, I felt, was impartial, yet fair.

Jeanette will find me like this—sitting in the pen, eyes closed, puppies "nursing" on my fingertips—and say, "Don't just sit there, get busy." Ha ha, Jeanette. It's the command—"get busy" is—for a guide dog to eliminate.

I often time my visits to when the older puppies are fed. A Labrador eating looks like time-lapse photography. After the pups have been weaned and are on to softened kibble, their food is set down for them in bowls like Bundt cake pans, a kind of circular trough. They crowd in around it and the pan begins to turn. It spins faster as they eat and push, until the pups are like propeller blades. Then they'll move in the opposite direction, and the bowl spins the other way, as though they are in the southern hemisphere. One of the staff put a cartoon on the wall: "Why dogs never survive shipwrecks." It's the captain dog standing up in a lifeboat addressing the other dogs: "Those in favor of eating all the food now, say 'Aye.' "

A beauty came in yesterday—Stella, out of Barnstormer Billy and one-eyed Tara. Stella will have an *A* litter (we name the litters alphabetically), so in the time I have left I write down the names in a tiny three-ring binder: Avalon, Ardor, Able, Axel. Jeanette looks over my shoulder and says, "Like Axl Rose? You don't look like a headbanger."

Acre. I was looking in the dictionary, and after "acre" it said, From the Latin *agere:* to lead.

In the afternoon: stairs—closed and open, up and down, on a short lead.

It is astonishing to find out how quickly the wrong things come into your head. I don't mean the vain thoughts that are unseemly and irrelevant in surroundings such as these. I mean that I can pause outside a kennel to dip my shoes in bleach and be visited by the memory of shattering glass, the way the etched glass of the heirloom globe exploded. I had lit a candle in the old lamp but had not fitted it carefully; as it burned, it tilted until it touched the handblown glass, handily prefiguring the news, over dessert, that my husband was going to get on with it because how long *was* a person supposed to give the other person to come back?

Last night, Stella delivered early. Nine healthy puppies, and one—the smallest, a female—with a cleft palate. She died within minutes. Fran, the staffer present at the whelp, entered it in her log, her notation including the name she gave this pup: Angel. There are those of us who seek Fran out in the hope that something of her rubs off. Fran helped Stella deliver over a period of seven hours. At midnight, when there had been three quiet hours, Fran helped Stella to her feet and ran the ultrasound scanner over the dog's belly. Nothing showed on the monitor, so Fran left the kennel to get some sleep. Yet in the morning when she checked in on the mother, there were ten healthy puppies nursing. During the night, Stella had given birth to one more, a female, as though to replace the one who had died. I said why didn't we name her "After," or put a little French on it—"Après"—but Fran said no, she wanted to name her for Angel. Sentimental? I am not the one to say; before I gave up Goodman, I made a tape recording of his snores.

Maybe it was fatigue, or the sadness of losing the runt, but Fran snapped at me when I showed up for work. She asked a perfunctory question. I should have said I was fine. But instead I observed that this was the day my husband left for Paris with his new girlfriend.

"Like you have a right to complain," Fran said, incredulous. "Let's think back one short year."

I was stung, and flushed, and fumbled at the sink. Did I expect sympathy? Browbeaten, yet subdued. Subdued, yet humbled. I left the room before she could say I didn't have a leg to stand on, or the shoe was on the other foot.

Back in the lounge, I wiped at the antibacterial wash

I had splashed on my jeans. What gets on my clothes here—if it came from a person I'd be sick. Last week I was in the infirmary when a Lab was brought in with the tip of his tail cut off by a car door. Yet he was so happy to see the veterinarian that he wagged his tail madly and sprayed us all with blood, back and forth, in wide arcs. The walls and cabinets too.

There is much to learn from these dogs. And we must learn these things over and over!

In the way that we know things before we know them, I dreamed that I swam across Lake Michigan, then pulled myself up on a raft near shore; just then the light changed in such a way that everything underwater was visible in silhouette, and giant hammerheads shadowed by. This was the night before my husband told me about Paris, and even in the dream I remember thinking, If I had known what was in the lake, I never would have gone in.

It's a warmish day for December, so I take one of the broods for a walk on the grounds. It's a lovely old neighborhood. Down the road from the school is one of those classic mansions you admire until you notice it's a funeral home. Every day I drive past it to get here, and an image undoes me, though I can't say quite why: a pair of white gloves folded over the wheel of an old Ford Fairlane outside a funeral home in Georgia in June.

The sight of geese has this effect on me too. The dogs scare them up from the pond. When my best friend and I were in the first grade, her father acquired a dozen German Embdens. He let them roam freely about the yard. Every evening when he came home from work, he would turn a hose on the droppings they left in the drive; the grass along both sides of blacktop was a stripe of vivid green. He was a little eccentric, and the first of my friends' parents to die.

Buddha, Baxter, Bailey, Baywatch. I throw in that last for Jeanette. Working a litter ahead. We don't name the pups until they are four weeks old and get their ears tattooed, but still, it's good to be ready.

Back in the lounge there are letters from a sister school in Canada that has taken several of our dogs who failed the qualifying exam—except we don't say "failed," we say the dog was *reassigned,* or *released* for adoption as a pet. Canada will take a "soft" dog, one who maybe startles or is a bit less independent. Maybe it is like William Faulkner not getting into the U.S. Army Air Force and then going to fly for Canada. What's *with* Canada?

Trying to smooth things over, I guess, Fran asks for a hand in putting together the invitation for the Christmas party. I make James Thurber look like da Vinci, but I stay late—it's the night of the six-months-and-under class, the babies—and work up a festive border. The party is a high point for the volunteers who raise the puppies. They bring them to the high school gymnasium we borrow, and dress them up in Santa hats or felt reindeer antlers held on with chin straps, and there are cookies for everyone, and in the center of the gym floor there is a large cardboard box filled with wrapped gifts. On the command, the volunteers walk their dogs, one at a time, up to the box, where the dog is allowed to reach in and select a present, then return in a mannerly way to his spot. They get excited, of course, and invariably there will be a dog, like Ivan last year, who will get to the box and jump in.

Everyone wants to know how you do it, how you raise a puppy and train it for a year and a half and then give it up. Because you don't just love the dogs, you *fall* in love with them. A love affair begins with a fantasy. For instance, that the beloved will always be there. But *these* love affairs begin with yearning, for a future that won't be shared. Good training. There is a Zen-like quality to this work, if you can find reward in staying in the moment and in giving up what you love because someone else's need is greater. Sounds good in theory, but I counseled a volunteer who was coming up on the separation and she was crying and angry, and she said, "Just because I'm not blind!" She said, "What if he never swims again? Swimming's his favorite thing." I said, "You know how dogs' paws paddle in their sleep?" Dreams: the place most of us get what we need.

There is another side to this; it makes a pretty picture. The folks who raise the pups and then have to give them up? When the dogs get old and retire, the raisers can get them back. They can take them back in their well-earned rest. Raise enough puppies over the years—a steady stream of dear ones returning home.

Fran doesn't hold a grudge. She says she liked the invitation, and we walk together to the office to have it copied.

There are people whose goodness brings them to do this work, and there are those of us who come here *for* it. Both ways work.

Although, metaphorically, I am still in the lake, priding myself on a strong Australian crawl while nearby a hammerhead waits. Never mind the fact that this ravenous shark, in real life, is found in warm seas. It is with me in the lake where I mourn my lost status as someone who doesn't cause problems, and prove again that life is one long medley of prayers that we are not exposed, and try to convince myself that people who seem to suffer are not, in fact, unhappy, and want to be persuaded by the Japanese poem: "The barn burned down. / Now I can see the moon."

Did I invite this? It is like sitting in prayers at school when the headmistress says, "Who dropped lunch bags on the hockey field?" and although you went home for lunch, you think, *I did, I did.*

2.

I picked up coffee in town, but skipped the doughnuts and scones; after fifty-two years, my body owes me nothing. I ran into a former neighbor at the deli. We were still dressed the same in barn jackets and jeans; we both worked at horse farms. Standing in line for coffee, she picked crumbs of rust off an old bulb digger that looked pornographic in her hand. My own rusted one was plunged to the hilt in a circle of tulips where I left it when I heard about Lynney.

Claire, the former neighbor, told me she hadn't known Lynne Markson was divorced. I said she wasn't, they weren't, who told her they were? She said, "I thought *she* did." She said they had run into each other in line at the Film Forum, and Lynne told her she only came into the city once a week now. Lynne told her the rest of the time she lived upstate near her husband. Claire said she thought that was an interesting slip: "near" instead of "with."

I told her it wasn't a slip, and the reason she was upstate started the week the dog showed up in my yard, the same week my husband moved out. I would find the dog curled under the forsythia in the morning, in a shallow dirt bed he had dug the night before. When I let my own dogs out in the yard, he would stand and stretch, then stay still while they sniffed at him. He was a beagle wearing a faded too-tight collar he would not let me close enough to remove.

He was terrified of people, so I was certain he had been abused. But he liked the company of the dogs; he made himself part of the pack. Each morning he followed my dogs from the front yard with its hill, where their tennis balls rolled away, down into the backyard, where the three of them pawed at holes in the garden rows, probably after the moles that ate the centers out of the melons.

My dogs are female, so of course I indulged the notion that he had selected my house to fill the male post just vacated by my husband, who had moved back to the city. I stayed at the beach with the dogs and filled out my share of paperwork to make the separation final.

The beagle was small enough to shimmy in under the cedar fence gate where rain had eroded a patch of dirt into a small trough. He had rolled in, shook himself off, and stayed. I put out a bowl of food for him twice a day, and kept a bucket filled with water in the shade from the wisteria. The only time I knew he left the yard was when I took my own dogs across the street to walk through the fields that end at Round Pond. He would trail us, letting their bodies brush his when they all chased rabbits and squirrels. He had the look of a harried executive; he carried himself, chest first, like a little mogul. So I called him Beagleman. "Get me Beagleman!" I would order my dogs. "I'll take a meeting in five minutes—*front* yard." And they would race off to get him and herd him into the front and we would file across the street, every day a parade.

I didn't bother to fill in the dirt beds that Beagleman dug, and that my own dogs copied. The yard was a yard—it had never been an even "carpet" of green. Mowing had always been my job, one I liked, but I did not go beyond that to what more was required: grading, fertilizing, sprinklers.

Starting early in the summer, I put Beagleman's bowl closer to the house. Then I sat on the outdoor steps without moving or looking at him while he ate. When he finished, I tossed a handful of crumbled cheese in his direction. He would follow the spray of cheese, eating a trail that led to my open hand where more cheese was offered. He would start toward me, then stop and pulsate and whimper. At that point I would toss him the cheese and try again later in the day.

In the evenings around six—this was in July when the

sand at the beach is so hot—I would load my two dogs into the back of the station wagon and drive to the ocean for a swim. Beagleman would wiggle under the closed gate and stand at the top of the driveway as I backed the car into the street. He would be there when we returned at dusk, and fit himself under the gate when the three of us had passed inside.

After an early spring of taking the marriage apart, I was glad to have every day the same. I did not ask much of myself; it was enough to keep a cutting garden watered and shop at a farm stand for tomatoes and basil, and baby eggplant to grill, and that white corn that needs just three minutes in hot water with milk. It was enough to conduct classes for young beginning and intermediate riders at the farm, to keep my dogs and sometimes myself reasonably groomed, and try to win over the beagle. I was mindful of the symmetry—trying to establish this creature's trust, having dispatched that of my husband.

This took us up through August.

Then, just before Labor Day, I kept the cheese in my hand. And Beagleman ate it, his eyes on mine. I told him he was a very good boy. He ate from my hand several times that day. I got him to follow me inside and into the kitchen, source of the cheese. I introduced him to a wall of cheese in the refrigerator. He ate from my hand while I gently touched his chin with a finger. I rubbed under his chin while he ate, and it was only another day before he let me rub his muzzle. From there it was his ears, scratching them while he sat beside me. I cut off the collar that left a dent in the skin of his neck.

At the end of the summer, he let me brush him while he rested his head on my leg. Within the week I had him upstairs, and we celebrated by having a slumber party— the three dogs up on my bed in the dark, eating popcorn and watching a movie.

Beagleman seemed to be proud of himself. He walked with confidence, he no longer hung back. He was in the front seat of the car on every errand. At night he raced ahead of me up the stairs; I would find him on my pillow on his back, waiting for me to rub his stomach.

This lasted until the lawyers said we would have to sell the house. I would be moving, I would be renting, and no one would rent to a person with three dogs. That was when I heard that Lynne Markson wanted a dog.

Back then, they had the place on the North Fork as well as the apartment on Riverside Drive. I arranged for Lynne and her husband, Whit, to visit.

Beagleman liked Lynney right away. He showed no fear, and I was proud of how far he had come. He was less comfortable around Whit. I had predicted this; he was still skittish around men, probably because a man or men had hurt him. Whit was gentle and welcoming, so we said: sleepover, trial visit. Beagleman sat in Lynney's lap in the car on the way to the city.

A few weeks later, Whit takes Beagleman out for an evening walk. As they are about to cross Riverside Drive,

Beagleman slips his leash and bolts into the street. Reflexively, Whit runs after him.

Lynne is at home when the confused doorman phones up to say her dog came back by himself. He tells her the dog walked right through the lobby and into the elevator, so he—the doorman—pressed the button for their floor and sent him up.

Lynne gets the dog inside, then runs out to find Whit.

She follows the sound of a siren, and finds him just as the ambulance pulls up.

Claire looked at me as though she had been watching a performance. Which she had. I could not tell the story enough times. An observant friend had remarked that "Those who can't repeat the past are condemned to remember it."

I realized I had left out the part about Christmas Eve when Beagleman got lost in Noyac. So I did not get to say, "If I had not driven back that third time—if I had gone to midnight mass instead." I did not tell Claire that Lynne does not blame the dog, or that the dog follows her from room to room and sleeps with his head on the pillow, in her bed, in the house where she lives near her husband, who lives in rehab.

Claire, my former neighbor, said she would write to Lynne if I would give her the new address. She said, "How's Lynney doing?" And I said, "It's *her* story now."

3.

I was the one who did the back and forth; he was the one who did the every which way. He would stop in the course of the walk and talk with a friend, or a not-even friend, someone he hadn't seen in a while, invite the person to breakfast or lunch, even if the person was more my friend than his. His invitation would be so open-faced that it would seem mean not to take it. Then he would want me to come along.

The people I stopped for when I walked the dog were strangers who wanted to pay the dog a compliment, or pay me one for having such a dog. An unusual mix that was hard to place, the dog was a maverick; she had attitude, she was willful and people responded to that. If she liked you, then you were worth liking. With the dog present, I could talk to people I could not have talked to without her.

The dog had been our second choice. My husband wanted the pretty one, and I had wanted to keep the runt. But we each picked the same runner-up.

I counted the blocks when I walked the dog, or the equivalent of blocks in the park. I liked to return the same way we had come. I walked the dog on the other side of the street, or the path, so she could have variety. But I liked things to be the same, to be where they were the last time I saw them, when I saw them for the last time.

4.

For sixty dollars charged to my MasterCard in advance, the psychic described a wooded area near a body of water—a pond? a stream? she couldn't be sure—with a view across an open field to a "civic-type building"—a post office? a school? she couldn't be sure—where, according to her vision as relayed to me over the phone, the lost dog had looked for food in the last twenty-four hours.

This was less useful than the woman down the turnpike who saw the leaflet left on her windshield. She phoned to say she had seen the dog drag a deer across the tracks a hundred yards away the day before. I found the dead deer beside the tracks where the woman said, part of its flank gnawed to the bone. The dog could not have felled the deer; it must have been hit by a train. Had an approaching train scared the dog from its food?

The leaflet is all over town.

The ex-husband made it.

He advertised a reward beside a picture of the dog. But he did not consult with me first. The reward would not buy you an ordinary dinner in this town. Whenever I come across any of his posters, I add a "1" before the amount.

Despite the reward, calls come in. I chase down all sightings, even when the caller says the collar is red, not blue. But there is never any dog of any kind with any color of collar in the spot reported by the time I am able to get there.

I check construction sites. Workmen eat lunch outdoors, and a hungry dog might try them for a handout, wouldn't she? Half a dozen calls come from builders on the beachfront. Once, when I got there, there was a deer swimming in the ocean. It appeared to be caught in the tide, and as I moved toward it—toward the deer—it managed to pull itself ahead of the surf, where it found its footing and limped ashore on a hurt front leg, to leap away when I moved closer. So I, who only wanted to help, was made to stand there watching the deer head for the dunes.

I went out again at night to lay down scent trails in the woods near my house, wearing the same shoes and socks I had been wearing for days. The moon was nearly full above a snowy field. When I had made my way into the woods, I turned and saw deer standing side by side, watching. I thought, Saints, guardian angels, my saviors, my friends.

We watched each other for a while, and then I went home, checking over my shoulder all the way for the deer. They never moved once—not that I saw.

There were three animal psychics.

I phoned them all.

The famous one you can't get to work with you anymore unless you're the president of something and your dog is, too. Still, this woman phoned me from the airport, she said, between flights. She gave me the names and numbers of the other psychics who found missing dogs. Where's the one who finds missing husbands?

I called the most psychic-sounding one first, who turned out not to be available until after the holidays. What holidays? Were there holidays?

I left a message for the next one, and the third psychic answered her phone and insisted we could go to work with no delay so long as I could describe my dog to her and recite the numerals of my credit card number.

The worst thought I had was, What if the dog was just here? Right where I was standing?

Every morning and every night there is a videotape I watch. The ex-husband made it when he was my husband. It was made when the dog had first come to us and seemed to be everywhere, shared everything, offering, offering.

I see the viewfinder swing wide across the lawn, one

of those panning shots you always find in movies, where the idea is to get everybody in the audience ready for what will presently be revealed—but only if everybody will just be very very good, and very very patient, and will wait, with perfect hope, for the make-believe story to unfold.

THE AFTERLIFE

When my mother died, my father's early widowhood gave him social cachet he would not have had if they had divorced. He was a bigger catch for the sorrow attached. He was kind, cultured, youthful, and good-looking, and many women tended to him. They cooked dinner for him, and sent their housekeepers to his Victorian near the Presidio Gate. My brothers were away in college, but I, who had dropped out of school, spent a good deal of time at the house.

Some of the women who looked after my father banked their right actions for later, I felt. One woman signed him up for a concert series, but it was a kind of music he didn't much like, and he had been at a concert—chamber music—the night my mother died.

One woman stocked his kitchen with candied ginger and snail shells and bottles of good red wine. I would prop bags of Oreos and Fig Newtons alongside so my brothers would find something familiar when they came home.

One woman sang to him; another, when he asked if she could sing, said, "If I were to sing, it would sound like talking louder." A couple of the women courted me as the best bet. There were shopping trips, lunches in their gardens, suggestions for cutting my hair. I was not used to that kind of attention, and seeing through it didn't mean I didn't also like it.

One woman was impatient with his mourning, another seemed excited by it. She didn't wear underwear when she came to visit; I knew because I heard her tell him. He told me she sent him pictures of herself naked; he was midwestern enough to be stunned.

The woman I liked—for a while she came over every night. She would get to his house when it was still light enough to see fog blowing down the street from the bay window in the living room. He would make her a drink in the kitchen, stirring in the Rose's lime juice with a chopstick from the Japanese take-out place. He would carry it in to where he had seated her on the toast-colored Italian couch in front of the fire. The house was a hundred years old, but the furniture was futuristic.

She was futuristic. She was forward-looking, although the past was what they had between them. Jane Stein had known my mother in college. She had married a friend of my father's, and then had not seen my parents since. She still lived in the Midwest, but not with her husband anymore. I had looked her up the month before when I was in Chicago. When I found out she was going to San

Francisco, I told my father to take her to dinner. On their second date, she arrived at the house with a black cashmere sweater for me—a "finder's fee," she said.

On their third date, the three of us went to dinner. Other of the women had wanted me along so my father could see them draw me out. Jane wanted me there because we thought the same things were funny. When my father complained about a nosy woman who detained him in the grocery store, Jane said, "That's the trouble with people in general—you have to run into them."

When I hung back a bit walking to the car, she said, "Take up space!" and pulled me along by the arm. The next week, she didn't mind that I saw my father walk her to the front door in the morning.

One night: "I made a fool of myself on that trip," I heard my father say. "Staying in the places I stayed with their mother years ago—I was posing the whole time," he said, "playing the part of a man in grief, from St. Petersburg to Captiva."

He was telling her about the time he'd gone by himself to Florida, only a few weeks after my mother died. Jane and my father were in the habit of travel. Every night they returned to his house, he mixed her a drink with a wooden chopstick, and took her on the trips he had taken to China, and Switzerland, and Venice with his late wife. Jane told him she would have thought she would be more interested in hearing about the places she had not seen herself, but was, in fact, more interested in where they had gone in this country, especially the places that she knew, too, along the coast of Florida. "What year was that?" she would ask, then do the math to see what she had been doing at the time.

When it was time for her to leave for the night, or the next morning, my father would put an object in her hands for her to take; he would divest himself of yet another *thing*—a Waring blender, a toaster oven—he could not imagine using again. He gave her classical CDs, a copper omelet pan, several crystal vases, a Victorian planter, a set of good knives, sweaters if the temperature had dropped the slightest bit, a comforter, books, a pumpkin pie he had made—he gave her something every day. Most of it she gave to the women's shelter she was in town to advise. Then she would reappear, note all that had been given up or given away—the travel, the glass stirrer for drinks—and let him return to a place she'd never been.

On the last night she visited my father, she asked him if the two of them might go somewhere together. And he said, "Darling, I don't go to the *dining room* anymore."

"Is there a place you *could* go and be happy?" she asked.

My father said that maybe he could go back to Aspen. That was where he and my mother, and sometimes we kids, went every summer for a handful of years. None of us were skiers, and in summer the town hosted a music festival in a huge tent set up in a meadow. World-class musicians filled small hotels, and swam in the pools with tourists like us. My father knew a lot about classical music, so he was happy discussing the afternoon program with the First Chair Violin while my mother read on a chaise in the sun, and my brothers tried to land on me in the deep end from the high board.

This was when we had lived in a suburb of Denver, and went rock-collecting weekends in the foothills. The lichen-covered rocks we brought back in the car ended up in the yard framing native flowering plants. I got to stay in the car and drink Tab after a rock I picked up freed something I still have dreams about. The mountains had nothing for me, and I did not yet know that *water* was going to be my place on earth, not swimming pools at small hotels, but lakes, the ocean, a lazy-waved bay, ponds ringed with willows, and me the girl swimming under low-hanging branches brushed by leaves for the rest of my days.

I heard Jane ask my father if he was happiest when he was in Aspen. He said, "I was, and then I wasn't." She said, "You can *was* again." He said he didn't think so. And she didn't come back the next day.

In a note to me a couple of weeks later, Jane wrote from Chicago that she would miss us. She said she understood that my father's life had ended with my mother's death, and that what he inhabited now was a kind of afterlife—not dead, but not alive to possibility, to what else one might still choose, and "Who would choose to live less?" she asked.

I didn't mention the note to my father, but I asked him if he wished she still came over. He said she was a terrific person.

The women that followed included a self-styled libertine, and a beauty whose parents had called in a priest to exorcise her when she was a child. Some of the women were contenders—generous, brimming, game.

The woman he sees now seems decent and kind. I met her at his house this morning. She was clearing his garden of weeds, advising him on the placement of a eucalyptus tree.

She left before I did. My father waved to her from the bay window, and asked if I didn't think she looked a little like Jane Stein.

I said, "That was a long time ago," and he said, so I understood him, "*Nothing* is a long time ago."

MEMOIR

Just once in my life—oh, when have I ever wanted anything just once in my life?

OFFERTORY

We did it twelve times—made love, all of us, to one another twelve times, the two of them doing everything two people could do to me twelve times. I was going to say only twelve times, but it wasn't "only," was it? It was wonderful.

I began, last night, at the beginning. The rule was I had to tell the truth, and I had to tell him everything. I could start where I liked. I told him the story every night; he asked for it, for some version of it, every night. Sometimes I left out a detail so he would prompt me, and thus participate after a fashion. "The inevitability of orgasm?" he might say, and I would say, "The way she moved her hip into me first."

Sometimes I changed their names. Names were not the details that mattered to him. What mattered was the most refined particularity of our actions, and the declarative nature of my narrative. He did not want me to use language that said anything other than what it was. For me, I mean. Well, for them, her. All of us.

"I want you to give me points on the body—nuanced, subtilized, exact," he said. "I want fine-grained diction in the reportage, and I want it to be plummy. I want the ring of inexpressible reality—yet lyric.

"Were there photographs?" he asked, knowing that there were.

"Tell me," he said he wanted to know, "who took the pictures of you?"

Sometimes I tried to tell a different story. But he liked best when I told him about the man and the woman together—together with me. I learned that the more *froideur* in my tone, the more heated, the more insistent he would become—until I would be unable to continue because his mouth would be stopped up.

"Don't let the game warden see you," said the man painting the dock. "Indians the only ones allowed to net fish."

The net I was sweeping through the shallow part of the lake was a child's butterfly net I had found in the sand. The dock painter who warned me against the game warden was the same dock painter who had told me that a black racer was a water moccasin. I didn't tell him I knew he was wrong, but let him think I was rash for reaching in after it.

People on the lake were ready with the rules, rebuked the fantasy daily. The vision had been: Swim with the dog, shoulder-to-shoulder, every morning, to the other side. But a hand-stenciled sign was posted when the season started: NO DOGS ON BATHING BEACH, though dogs were not the nonreaders leaving Band-Aids and cigarettes in the water.

The seven hundred dollars I had paid in dues covered plowing snow, but I would not be getting the benefit of winter. I had moved here for the lake, and then would not go in the lake; I'd be gone before leaves began to fall.

The former tenant said she had recovered here. From what, she did not say, but she said she had given herself five years to do it in. Well, was there anybody who wasn't here to get over something, too?

His letter was forwarded to me here.

"I believe I need another look at someone who writes such a charming letter," he said.

I had written to him after our meeting two years before. I had told him everything in that letter as though he had asked for me to. I had written him the whole time I was away, a woman he had met just once. And then he wrote me back. He invited me to see his new work. He had a show opening soon, he said, and the paintings were not, he said, anything like what he had done before.

He said he liked the way I described the place where I had been, where the small group of us lived, and got better. He said he liked the sound of the beach where we went when we were given a pass. He said he had tried to paint such a place, and maybe I would like to see it.

*   *   *

I had twenty years to go to get to be as old as he was, and then, if I got there, I'd have to go counting almost twenty years again. I was still in my thirties, but I was the one of us who was old. Anyway, he said he was nostalgic for my past.

I had a past, and my past contained a marriage and a job and friends. But I had long since dispensed with this past. I had spent the year before moving to the lake at a place where people recover from the bad things that seek them out. For the time I was there, I wrote to this man although, or because, I had met him only once, and because I felt our talk had been not an exchange of words, but of souls.

I read about a famous mystery writer who worked for one week in a department store. One day she saw a woman come in and buy a doll. The mystery writer found out the woman's name, and took a bus to New Jersey to see where the woman lived. That was all. Years later, she referred to this woman as the love of her life.

It is possible to imagine a person so entirely that the image resists attempts to dislodge it.

I lived in small rooms with heaps of bleached shells on distressed white tables and antique mantels. His place had the original brick arches between the large open areas of the loft. There were polished wood floors (slate in the kitchen and bath), and a frosted glass–and–steel screen hid the staircase to the upper bedroom. His paintings were hung in the enormous studio on the first floor, the range represented by portraits and landscapes following the early "systems" paintings. There were ordinary workday scenes supported by strict and intricate organization that a critic had commended as "art that conceals art."

Lying in bed early on: "We had rules," I reminded him. "I could fuck the wife anytime I wanted. I could fuck the husband if the wife was also present. The wife could, whenever she wanted, fuck either one of us—her choice: together or alone. The husband needed no rules, both we women felt, because, we also seemed to feel, we would have no idea where to start in the drawing up of them.

"They took me up," I told him. "I was young," I reminded him. As if he, of all we did, needed reminding!

"Which of you would make the first move?" he asked.

"The first time or any time?" I asked.

"Maybe the wife started it?" I said. "Maybe the first time she made a preemptive strike? Maybe she saw the way her husband was looking at me—I guess she made up her mind to beat him to it? You know, later on she told me that was exactly what she was doing."

"Tell me what you had on," he said, "the first time, and every time."

"The wife said any dress looks good in a heap on the floor by the bed."

He said he wanted me to tell him about myself and about the woman when the two of us were in bed before the husband came home, how we would not let him join us at first, but let him crouch beside the bed, his eyes at the level of our bodies on the mattress, first at the side of the bed, and then at the foot of the bed. And who had undressed first—had we undressed each other?

"Would you do anything—everything—they wanted?" he asked, although the real question was, Would I do everything with *him*?

Let him find out!

"It wasn't always like that," I said. "Sometimes we just let the cats sleep in the bed."

"Oh?" he said. "Did they come into it in some way? There was cat hair in the sheets? On the two of you? On the three of you?

"And did you like to be watched?" he prompted. "Did you like it more when she watched you with him, or when he watched you with her?"

"Don't forget the neighbors," I said. "The couple who watched at the window where the curtains didn't close all the way. The man I didn't mind, but I thought the woman wanted to take my place, and I felt she resented me for it."

"You had never done anything like this before?" he said.

"I saw no reason not to."

"It was the great experiment," he said. "Did you wait until evening? Often you couldn't wait."

"That's true," I said. "I was supposed to be available."

"Every day," he said, "they touched you every day? Even on Sundays—you made yourself available to Saturday night's predations?"

"All the better," I said. "The better it was, the better it was."

"You mean the more, the more of them?" he said.

"Repetition fueled us," I said.

In the bed where I described the couplings years ago, he would suddenly roll me over so that I was on top. He would tell me to lean over and show him how my hair had made a tent over the face of the husband or of the wife.

The enclave at the lake had begun as a German settlement. The original developer built cabins for his family, and more cabins for their friends. The row of mailboxes at the end of Valkyrie Drive still featured mostly German names.

After an evening in the city, downtown, I would drive myself at dawn up the parkway and back to the lake. Before going to bed for a couple of hours, I would walk the dog through the woods and up the small mountain that is the backdrop for the place. At a point near the top, on the edge of an overlook, are the two cedars the German founder planted to stand for himself and his wife.

There were motion-sensor lights throughout my yard, and the few nights I was there, all night animals set them off. My heart used to race at the thought of intruders, but then I would see the doe nursing a fawn not many feet from a window, or a procession of bucks crossing the front yard to drink from the lake. So I came to look forward to these sudden illuminations.

Replacing lightbulbs, taking out trash, watering plants: exigencies of the tiny life, a life that opened up inside me at night in a downtown loft on an ugly street in a city rebuilding itself.

It started up with us at the place we went for dinner after leaving his friend's opening at a gallery in Chelsea. I had strained to say something kind, and he had pointed out the flaws in the artist's logic; he criticized the concept as well as its execution, and was not wrong.

His voice, doing so, was—sophisticated. It was a young man's voice; it was dignified and persuasive, and made me feel like an accomplice. Under the words, his voice seemed to say, "You and I are looking at this together, and we see the same thing." When I could keep up with him, that was true.

We walked easily together; I leaned into him, my head almost to his shoulder.

He continued the analysis over dinner, and as we were finishing, he said, "What if one told every truth! Recorded the most evanescent reactions, every triviality, an unimpeded account of lovers' minute-by-minute feelings about the other person: Why didn't she order the braised beef the way I did? She raved about the sea bass, wrongly. I set my watch three minutes fast; she set it back."

Here he took us into the future—he reached across the table to stroke my hair. "And I'd say, 'What about her hair across the pillow? I had thought it would be finer.' "

His stance was not unlike the one I had proposed to him in my letter, that we observe the Wild West practice: We put our cards on the table.

We moved into what he called "the precincts of possibility," of anything-goes, of nothing undisclosed.

He wanted to hear "cock" and "cunt," but I was more likely to want to show him what the man and woman did to me all those years ago. He had told me to say we did it twelve times. Did what? What we did, well, wouldn't that be up to me? Didn't it have to?

I told him what they did to me the first time, and the second, and the third through the eighth and ninth— some nights I teased him: "That's it. I can't remember the rest. Sorry. Only remember nine."

But he was persistent, encouraged me to continue, to

THE DOG OF THE MARRIAGE

say more, to remember, to get it right. And when I really could not remember what happened the tenth time, I made something up. I made up something I guessed would be what he wanted. For example, he wanted to know when the husband was with both of us at once, whose name did he cry out when he came? He asked for the tenderest time, the most violent time, the most non-chalant time, the classiest time, the first time and the last time, all twelve times.

"And everyone was the better for it?" he said with admiration. "You were each made to feel more your-selves?"

"Of ourselves," I said.

I was never more myself than when I was lying in this man's arms. But was I ever much *of* myself in them?

"Don't you ever get jealous?" I asked.

"Of course I do," he said. "I admit to ineluctable jealousy—comparisons, comparisons, real and imagined. And, as it happens, there exists in me—not pathologically, but all too humanly, I think—a species of delight arising from this knowledge. Darling," he said, conspiring, "are these conflicting sentiments and the mystery they point to not at the core of our alliance?"

The town whose main street ends at the river draws tourists who come to shop for antiques. The prices aren't bad, and the town is picturesque and you can walk off the train and be pricing iron garden chairs before you've caught your breath. Boaters wave from the river that is, at this point, miles across. But the Jet Skis are annoying, and dogs are not allowed on the restored promenade. I had been there just long enough for the owner of the delicatessen to know how I took my coffee, and to avoid the speed trap on the other side of the bridge.

There was a backup generator on the north side of my house. It kicked on on its own once a week at noon, startling me each time. It ran for a while to give the impression it would be in good working order when it was really needed. An engineer down the road explained it to me; he said that during a snowstorm mine would be the only house with lights and heat. He told me not to use more than two appliances at a time.

"You'll have all your neighbors coming over to get warm," he said to me, either believing the observation a comfort to me or a threat.

I filled the dog's water bowl about half the way full. I set it back on the porch. I could use a larger bowl, but I would rather the dog see me fill it many times in a day, see me think of her needs and move to meet those needs oh so many times each day.

Sleepy from the night before, I watched the kid from the next town mow my lawn in half the time it took me the times I did it. He charged very little. I would see him being careful out back where he would circle the maple tree not to nick the metal grave marker with the German name of a woman and the date of her birth and the date of her death. Ashes, I had guessed, but forgot to ask the owner.

That night in bed in the bed downtown, I said, "I know you don't know anything about ashes or lakes, but is it legal—can you put someone's ashes anywhere you want to?"

"There is no lake," he said, the words slurred against my neck. "There are only the two domains: this bed, and the bed of memory. Get rid of the lake," he said. "Two people can go anywhere they want to go right here."

I was never late.

By eight o'clock, he would already have ordered dinner for us. The sushi would be delivered in an hour, and left by the door.

Some nights we did not make it past the entryway before dinner arrived. Some nights he would close the door and then press me against it, or against a wall, and hold me there until we dropped to the polished wood floor together—we would not have said anything to each other. And we would stay there until we heard the brush of the delivery man outside.

When we finished dinner, he would put on music for us, something he had looped to play over and over again, a piece he had chosen or something he knew I liked, something we both liked to hear behind us.

Then he would be inside me again so quickly I was, each time, surprised.

Kissing my eyes, he said, "Did Phillip start like this?"

And that night the husband would be Phillip.

The first time I went to see him at the loft, I found something he didn't drink in the kitchen. I didn't like it either, and on subsequent visits I checked to see if the level of juice in the bottle was lower, if the juice-drinker had been to see him. This changed the night I told him about the twelve times. He asked me to come back the next night, and the next. Each time I looked, I saw that the level of juice was the same. That is when the place became a sanctuary for me, and which of us does not need sanctuary all the time?

I tried to remember what I had told him the time before. That Katherine—I was calling the wife "Katherine"—took me home after taking me to lunch at a grimy place in China Basin, a fishermen's supply shop that sold bait next to the coffee and doughnuts you could take out onto a dock and eat while oil tankers got overhauled.

"Did she want you to undress? Or did she want to undress you herself?" he wanted to know. He was twisting my hair as he spoke. He could not braid it with only one hand, so he twirled it around his fingers and let it spring loose again.

"Show me how she kissed you," he said.

I kissed him in a way I imagined Katherine might have done.

He said, "When you kiss me like that, my heart is so stolen."

Back at the apartment, he patted himself down.

"It must have slipped out of my pocket in the theater," he said, "when I reached over to button your coat."

I said, "Why don't you call the theater and ask them to check our row."

The book was a rare one. He had underlined parts throughout.

He returned to the kitchen to make the call, and—"Oh! Oh, look! I must have taken it out without thinking," he said of the book there beside the stove.

And when the phone rang, he said, "That must be the theater calling, to tell us the book has been found."

It was midnight when we removed the clear covers from the containers of densely packed sushi. He could not stand the green plastic fences that separated one kind from another, so I removed them and removed the ginger as well. I mixed soy sauce with the wasabi. I would have eaten from the containers, but he arranged the pieces in a pattern on good china.

We watched the late news while we ate the tuna and salmon. When he had cleared the plates and turned off the television, he asked me to put my black dress back on.

He led me to the leather club chair near the bed. He sat down first, and brought me to him so that I faced him. He pushed the black dress up to my waist and pulled me somewhat roughly onto his lap.

"Did Phillip feel left out?" he asked, moving slowly inside me.

I told him that after a couple of weeks of going out with just Katherine, the three of us went to a party. I told him we drank and drank and then went to their house late. "Phillip got out his camera," I said, "and attached a different lens. He said, 'Show me what the two of you have learned about each other.' "

"Those pictures," my lover said, gripping my shoulders. "Where are they now? You have to get me those pictures.

"Ask Phillip for those pictures," he said, out of breath.

When he had me: the word "slown."

It was a thing between us—*slown*. One night I heard him say on the phone, "We were stoned, or I was stoned, and she said, 'You hear what you said?—you just said *slown*.' That was nice. It was nice, the way she heard me say it wrong and then went ahead and made it a thing between us—the word *slown*. 'Time has slown down.' It was like this woman was getting just as slown down as I was, even though she never touched the stuff. It was honor, it was allegiance. It had an effect on us—the word."

I listened to him talk to his friend, and, happy, went into his kitchen. I got silver polish and a rag from under the sink, and contentedly polished a pair of candlesticks.

Cast-iron bookends with embossed baskets of flowers on them—these are a morning's find on Main Street. The shops sell mirrors with milk-painted frames; I've bought several of them for gifts, but not for him. I am not allowed to bring him anything but myself. He has returned gifts to me the times I disobeyed ("We do not quite forgive a giver"), and I gave those things away.

Not lewd, not urbane, not leering or concupiscent, but *devotional*. That is how I felt about Katherine and Phillip, and about the man I offered them up to. He looked for jolting carnality, for physical imperatives. "Didn't more rules appear with a certain periodicity?" he wanted to know.

We were awake in the night, in the early morning, really. I had been lying still, rubbing a finger on the mended spot on the sheet where hydrogen peroxide had made a hole when he rubbed at a spot of blood—not mine. He got out of bed to turn off the air conditioner, and wrapped himself around me when he returned. With no need of a segue from my hurried-off clothes on the floor, I said, "I can't remember—does the week in Acapulco count as one time?"

"I want *each* time in Acapulco," he said, as I knew he would.

I gave him a familiar travelogue just to see how long until he'd interrupt with "Cut to the chase—the beach, the waves, sunset, dinner, you're back in the house in bed."

I pushed him off me so that he could come back even closer.

"We chose a room with a skylight above the bed. It was smaller than the other bedrooms in the rented house, but we wanted to see the stars. Phillip would not be joining us for another day or two, so the mood was hen party, sorority house."

He moved steadily inside me, so wonderfully inside me as I spoke. When he asked me a question, he spoke into my mouth. I had to turn my head and tell him to repeat it in my ear.

He smoothed his hand down my silk camisole and asked me if I needed to be coaxed. "Did you reach for Katherine first?"

"Not then, maybe not ever," I said. "It was not a lack of desire," I told him. "I took an active part by setting desire in motion. To be in a condition of readiness is to participate fully," I said. "As I am now."

"Show me what she did to make you come that night," he said.

In showing him, I took him to the other side of himself.

A short time later, he pulled me down to the thick carpet in front of the tall oval mirror. He put a pillow beneath my head, and another under my hips. He said, "When Phillip arrived, did the three of you spend that night in the room with the skylight?"

In fact, I remembered pleading exhaustion that night, and sleeping by myself downstairs. But there was nothing for him in that. I gave him instead a scene from a live act I watched through a one-way mirror in a South-of-Market theater. Phillip had taken me there on a night when prohibitions turned into permissions. Neither of us had told Katherine.

I dressed for him on the night that made it a month since I had started meeting him at the loft downtown where he waited for me "all pins-and-needle-y," he said.

I had had to go to a dinner first, a benefit for something worth giving money to. The transition was too quick, the way it is when you fly to a place that you need train time to adjust to. On the way to the loft, I had felt tired by what went on there, by the bottomless pit of it, the ever-ratcheted-up attempts to hold his attention on me.

In the bedroom there was a movie playing. I recognized it as one of the red-boxed collection in his bedroom closet. We had watched this one before, the one in which the male star auditions Polish girls for his next film.

OFFERTORY

Were they really in Poland in the film? Who could tell?
What mattered was that these were girls who would do
anything, anywhere.

I arrived during the scene where the two girls, maybe
nineteen years old, are lying naked beside each other in a
hotel room. The star opens one girl's legs, and then the
other's, for the camera. Both of the girls have shaved, or
have been shaved. Then the star pulls the first girl, the
blonde, into a sitting position on the edge of the bed and,
standing in front of her, forces his cock into her mouth. It
is possible that the scene is, to some extent, unacted—the
size of his cock forces tears into the girl's eyes.

When the actor is finished with her, he turns to the
second girl, who has been watching him with the first. He
turns her over so that he can fit himself into her from
behind; at the same time, another man (he had been
lounging in a chair earlier, naked) pulls her on top of him
and enters her from the front. While this is going on, the
first girl wipes her eyes and breathes with her mouth open
as she watches the girl beside her on the bed. After a
while, the second girl cries out in Polish.

"The thing about these films," he said, "is that this
really happened. We're seeing something that really
happened."

I tried to rally to the feel of his hand on my leg. But
a part of me was still at the dinner, greeting guests in
black tie.

"You know why I want to see you with another

lover?" he said, watching the screen. "I want to see a secret you—I would trade possession of you for it."

He had offered to bring in women who modeled for him, and I had declined. I knew there was no one he would rather see me with than Katherine.

I thought of the photographs he had taken of me. He felt the results were not worthy, did not resemble the nature of what was. He said, "They do not convey the trance you occupy during those times, the trance both of us inhabit, one with the other, one on account of the other, during those times."

"So what is seen is not what is felt?" I asked.

He said, "No instrument carried from a prior place could be expected to capture the feelings effected there."

I had already found the photographs he'd taken of others in a portfolio in another part of the loft.

The moment I wished he would turn off the movie, he muted the sound and turned his attention to me. This quality of attention righted things between us.

Then we were all flesh, and all feeling in that flesh. We abided in it, joined and rejoined, distance collapsed.

"Harmony," he whispered.

I said the word back to him.

Harmony sought, harmony required, "No life lost to us," he said.

* * *

There is an almost unbridgeable gulf between what an artist sees and what an artist paints. I knew this from my studies, and from looking at things myself. There are artists—Mondrian was one—who went from representation to abstraction by painting dying flowers, chrysanthemums in Mondrian's case. With this man, it had happened in reverse. He had painted vases of dying asters, all the time getting closer to figuration. Early on, he gave me a drawing from this series, not the one I wanted, but the one he wanted me to have.

He told me not to bring him flowers, but I often brought flowers with me, lately cabbage roses. He seemed pained to receive them and did not really look at them until they started to decay. He could not wait to get rid of them so he could enjoy remembering them.

Renoir told Matisse he would pick flowers in the fields and arrange them in a vase, and then he would paint the side he had not arranged.

On the walls of the loft there were portraits of this man's mother, drawn while she lay in her hospital bed; he drew her as she got smaller, up until the day she died there.

"No one tells me better stories," he assured me. I was aware of the point at which a compliment becomes a trap, because you are expected to keep doing the thing you are praised for; resentment will follow when you stop.

"Lie back," I said.

That night I had worn my grandmother's diamond earrings. I thought I might leave one behind in his bed the next morning. The moment this occurred to me, I thought, Why should he require an object to bring me to mind?

The music he had put on was a medieval motet. Two voices begin, and are joined by two more, then two more, until forty-eight singers are holding forth together. It has the hypnotic effect of chant, but it is song. I knew that if he ever heard this music out in the world, I would be the person he would think of. There it was again, thinking in terms of souvenirs, what you take away from a place to help you call it back.

Obediently, he lay back in the barely lit room. I kept on a sea green slip and joined him, sitting on the bed so as to force his legs apart. I stroked him slowly and said, "The time in the pool at night? There was something I left out before."

"This was in Laguna?" he said, as though he could have forgotten.

"Katherine and I drove down in a day. We left at dawn and took the Grapevine south—not much to see, but we wanted to make the best time. I wanted to watch the sunset from her sister's pool, or, if we were too late for that, to see the full moon from the pool. We only stopped at that place that has the oysters."

"I know that place—"

"That's the one," I said.

"Her sister lived in one of those heavily landscaped compounds where several bungalows share a large pool. Night-blooming jasmine was planted around this pool, so the air smelled good when you swam after dark."

"You wear jasmine sometimes when you come to me," he said.

"We both gave in to the drone of the drive, that line down the center of the state. It was driving with a destination, but with nothing required of us when we got there."

"The way you can drive in California!" he said. "I used to love that about it."

I reached for a bottle of almond-scented oil. I poured a little in my hand.

"We didn't unpack at first," I said. "We pulled on bathing suits from a duffel bag and wrapped beach towel sarongs around them. Except that I had been unable to find mine, and had packed a leotard instead, the Danskin kind with the narrow straps, flesh-colored.

"There were only two other people in the pool. Two men were doing laps in the deep end. Katherine and I stood in water up to our breasts and held on to the edge of the pool with our arms stretched out behind us. The water was heated, and it swayed against us slowly from the motion of the swimmers doing laps."

"Time was slown way down," he said, his eyes closed.

"We stayed like that," I said, "until the men climbed

out of the pool and lay down on chaises spread with towels at our end.

"Are you with me?" I asked.

"Darling," he said.

"Katherine churned the water around her, and when
she did a handstand, I saw that she had taken off her suit.
The men saw, too, of course. They were quite a bit older
than we were, and wore plaid swimming trunks. What an
awful word—trunks.

"Are you listening?" I asked. "Because one of the
things I just told you was a lie. Can you tell me what was
the thing that I made up?"

"You mustn't tease an old man."

"But really," I said, suddenly exhausted, "don't you
have something like this on video? Maybe we could just
watch that?"

My voice was raw, and when I coughed, he got up to
get me a glass of water. On his way back from the
kitchen, he stopped to play back messages left by callers
during the night.

We were not much for dreams. But one I woke him up
to tell him went like this:

"I'm driving on a bridge."

"Transition," he said.

"When my car breaks down."

"You have a breakdown," he said.

"And suddenly the water is rising."

"Feelings," he said, "rising," he said.

"Your car needs a tune-up," he said, and drew me back to bed, where the Nice Man made the Bad Dream stop.

Sometimes he would reminisce about another woman. When I was chilly because I suspected the woman had been to the loft the day before, he would say, "Oh, come on. Now, come on. What does that take away from you?"

"Dignity?" I said. "I find it humiliating."

"You said in your letter that humiliation brings the softness of heart that allows you to listen to God."

"If you believe in God," I said.

"Or in humiliation," he said.

And when I grabbed a stack of photos of another inamorata and made a spray of them across the bed, he refused to speak to me for nearly a month.

During that time I caught up on sleep and made the acquaintance of whatever turned up in the woods. I tutored some of the kids at the lake in drawing. I swam with the dog after dark. One night we followed a woman in a bathrobe down the lane to the little beach. She dropped her robe in the sand, and walked naked into the water. I didn't hear a splash, and I didn't see her again. But the robe was gone in the morning.

When the month had passed and we broached the borders of accord, we went to a screening of a documentary film about the life of an artist he used to know. Why this painter had had to go and kill himself was the least of the mysteries about him. He had had a lively sense of fairness; the film director interviewed a patron who had balked at the asking price of a new canvas, and suggested he pay the artist three-quarters of the price instead. The artist agreed, and shipped his patron the painting with one-fourth of the canvas cut out.

On the way to the theater we had reviewed the movie rules: He said there was to be no talking, no eating, no touching, and that if I needed to cross my legs I was to cross them in his direction. Before the lights dimmed, he had tucked his sweater up under my chin and around my shoulders. Soon, both his arms were around me. His lips brushed mine on the way to whisper in my ear. He said my composure was remarkable. He said, "It is your forbearance we have to thank for what could be a new tranquillity." He said he believed life could be, if we would strive for composure, "all affirmation."

"Are you happy?" he asked me. It was a serious question. He meant, Was I happy sitting beside him about to start up again?

I touched his face.

"Then let us go and consecrate the desecrated ground."

*   *   *

On the night his best friend died, he said, "Stay with me."

It was almost morning and we had not slept and had not let go of each other all those hours, and he said quietly, "Stay with me."

I said, "You know I will."

He said, "You know what I mean."

I did know. He meant not all the time, but *for* all time. He meant despite everything he would do that would make me want to leave.

I said, "I know what you mean, and you know I will."

The dog disappeared.

For days I did what a person does when her dog has disappeared. No one at the lake had seen her. No one found a collar. I showed up crying at the loft days later. He walked me into the part of the loft where he worked. I saw that he had hung a new painting. It was a scene of Central Park on a sunny summer day. I saw a dog, as I had described my own to him, painted into the park.

"She came here," he said.

I didn't know what my neighbors at the lake thought of me, out all night and coming home just after dawn, walking a dog and then not walking a dog, not showing up for potlucks or Flag Day. But I kept the lawn mowed and put a flag decal on my car.

He asked about the place on the lake but he never came to see it. He had done all the traveling he was ever going to do; that was the impression he gave. Now he traveled in time, taking me with him to where he had gone when he was a go-er. I was not so eager to go any-where, really, so this didn't bother me, except for once when I thought we should drive to Maine. I wanted us to drift in a canoe across a calm, cold lake, and listen to loons.

He had been to a lake in Maine with someone else years before. He said his Maine had been a week at a famous fishing camp whose pricey guides took your family out at dawn and then fried your catch for lunch. What occupied him now was seeing how far a person could go in the realization of pleasure, without leaving home, two people in a bed.

"Where do you look first?" he asked, holding me from behind. "What do you look at first?"

He stood behind me after putting on a film. We looked at it together. In this one, a series of couples was glimpsed by a woman who made her way alone through a villa. There were no closed doors in this villa, so she kept finding men and women, or women and women, lying on beds or lounging in chairs naked. Those people were pleased, were excited, to have the woman see them. It seemed a good bet that one of those couples would invite the woman to join them.

His question was not rhetorical. He wanted to know what I looked at first. What anyone looked at first. His was a life of looking—he was an artist, and he said he wanted to see it all. I disappointed him. I did not know what I looked at first. The people onscreen were less interesting than what he was doing with me.

He kept the sound turned off. I was able to make him look away.

He said he wanted to see everything, but did he, really? Does a person want to know the thing he is asking you to tell him?

I wanted to get his voice on tape. I wanted to ask if he would mind repeating something he had said, this time into a microphone set on Record. The way he said "Darling," for example, with all seriousness. I would want to hear him say this over and over, the way he looked at the photographs he took of us in bed "to preserve our best behavior," he said, "against the times we are estranged and there is no one to divine our souls and pick us out from the rest."

The moment this would occur to me, I would feel a spur in my side, like the anxious spur of misalignment just before the two of us would subside into each other. I would kiss him roughly then, and he would kiss me back, and when we had fulfilled ourselves, we would fall asleep together. Waking later—I would wake up because he had—he would turn on the television and we would hold each other and watch the current events, "just lying still," he would croon, "while the world worlds up at us."

I had not heard from Katherine for many years when her forwarded letter reached me. She was coming to New York, and she said she wanted to see me. I did not think this was coincidence; I felt I had conjured her by talking about her every night. I was excited and panic-stricken. I wanted to show them off to each other, and that would be a disaster. The three weeks' notice had shrunk to a couple of days. I left a message at her hotel to hold for arrival.

Last night I found him looking at Raphael's *Alba Madonna*.

He held the book so I could see. "Why is she facing left instead of right?" he asked. "Why the triangular arrangement of figures? Why a river in the background? Why is she wearing red?"

"Because a human being made this?" I said.

"Because a human being made this," he said, pleased.

The window shades were up. I looked across the way to a window that was covered in sheer white fabric. The room was lit behind it so the woman in the room threw a visible silhouette. She was posing, or maybe doing a kind of yoga. Then a man joined the woman and she turned out the light.

"This dress is very beautiful," he said, his arms around me.

"An old gift from Katherine," I said. The seamstress had done a good job on the vintage navy lace. I had asked her to give it a lighter look by removing the silk lining from the knees down.

"I want to hear about your friend," he said, undoing the hooks and eyes. "But first I want to fuck you on this couch," he said.

"You do give it a gentlemanly contour," I said, by way of welcome.

"Are these tears?" he asked, smoothing hair back from my forehead.

"It's better in French."

"What is?" he said.

I told him the part of a poem I was thinking about, one I'd had to learn in school in French as well as English: ". . . From hope and fear set free, . . . / . . . even the weariest river / Winds somewhere safe to sea."

"You're going to meet Katherine," I said.

"It's brilliant," he said, "liberating the past for a revival in the present."

His questions about Phillip had been abandoned some time back, but he started up again about Katherine and me. He suggested I bring her with me the next time I came to the loft. Well, of course he did. I said I thought

« 129 »

we might do better in a gallery instead, with objects between us to look at, as we had. I knew he would be winning when I made the introductions. Katherine would be appreciative and intelligent and unimpeachably cordial to him. She might take a camera from her bag and take our picture, his and mine, then hand the camera to him to take one of her with me.

One kind of woman would phone him the next day. He would want to be helpful, and what would begin in passion and deceit would wind down to something ordinary. It would fill my mouth with stones. But maybe Katherine would do this too? Would Katherine require his gaze?

"Tell me again—"

Call-and-response.

Such an extravagant sense of what is normal. Depends on what you're used to, I suppose.

All those questions, each one of them a version of just the one thing: Was I better served in another's embrace than in his own?

"We might clear a space," I said. "You can't fill every hour."

"Is that what we've been doing?"

I never wanted to tell him.

He wanted his suspicion confirmed, although it would be ghastly to have it confirmed. I watched his salacity turn to fear. All the nights I had drawn out the exchange, holding back information, scornful of his boyish need to know, yet protective of that boyishness, too—his insatiable urging, wanting the savor of the way women are with each other, what they say to each other, him begging for female truth.

"May I count on you to utter the next sentence?" he would say.

I never wanted to tell him. I said, "I'll show you what she did to me," and he said, "But you can't show me, I'm not a woman—you have to tell me."

He was eager for the thing that would undo him. He had disallowed my earlier squeamishness, insisted I tear it apart. Okay. I would give him some female truth. What would have made me seem compliant when we started was assault by the time I told him.

I told him in just one word.

I said, "The answer to your question is: Precision. I can tincture it with more patently sexual language, but really, that's what you're after. Katherine was precise. I mean what you think I mean."

He looked me over to see if I was playing.

A thrilling calm settled over me.

He propped himself up on an elbow.

"Look at that," he said. "The single word that brings an inquisition to an end."

I leaned back on the couch and let my breath out. I held his hand and thought, What now? Not asking him, but myself.

Because it was up to me!

I would not introduce him to Katherine; I would not give him the chance to tell me she was more beautiful than he had imagined. Let him reside in his failure of imagination; I had been generous. I had more. But it was mine.

I led him from the couch back to the desecrated ground. I lay down next to him. I wanted to console him—I sent a herd of words and the dust rose and it was not enough.

He had told me to say we did it twelve times.

Well, maybe it was twelve times, and maybe it wasn't any times at all.

You want the truth and you want the truth and when you get it you can't take it and have to turn away. So is telling a person the truth a good or malignant act? Precision—that was easy. He had asked for it! There was more to tell; there would always be more to tell. If I chose to tell him.

In the meantime.

I was never more myself than when I was lying in this man's arms.

We lay quietly, holding each other. Time was slown way down. Finally he said, "Did you ever wear a linen dress on a summer day? A wheat-colored linen dress whose hem fluttered in a breeze? And did you pin up your hair on both sides so that your long hair funneled down your back in that breeze?"

I did not know who he was describing, but I said yes,

I had dressed like that in the summers when I was young.

"Darling," he said.

I knew he was not entirely with me, and I had a shopworn thought: To be able to reverse the direction of time! But wouldn't we have to go through the same things in reverse?

"Darling," he said again.

So here we go, careening along in the only direction there is to go in, our bodies braced for transport—"Unimprovable," he says.

NOTES

Page 35–36: The harpist who sings at the bedside of the dying is the musicologist and thanatologist Therese Schroeder-Sheker.

Page 63: The expert who defined animal happiness is Vicki Hearne.

Page 77: "Those who can't repeat the past are condemned to remember it" is from Mark O'Donnell.

Page 102: The mystery writer is Patricia Highsmith.

Page 114: "We do not quite forgive a giver" is from Ralph Waldo Emerson's essay "Gifts."

Page 123–24: The artist is Ray Johnson, in the film *How to Draw a Bunny.*

Page 129: The lines quoted are from "The Garden of Proserpine" by Algernon Charles Swinburne.

ACKNOWLEDGMENTS

Deepest thanks to my editor, Nan Graham, and to my agent of 25 years, Liz Darhansoff. And to Pat Towers, friend and supporter for nearly that long. I am most grateful to the Guggenheim Foundation for a Fellowship in 2000, and to Elaina Richardson, who was so generous with crucial time at Yaddo. My thanks to the staff of the Guiding Eyes for the Blind Whelping Center in Patterson, New York—especially Linda Hines and Fran Midgley—and to Jane Russenberger, Director of the Breeding Center.

My thanks to Bill Wegman and Christine Burgin for the cover photograph. My thanks to Sheila Kohler and Bill Tucker for their generosity and support. I want to acknowledge the various kinds of help I received from Jill Ciment, Norah Cross, Robyn Fields, Lynn Freed, Martha Gallahue, Fiona Maazel, Pearson Marx, Rick Moody, Kathy Rich, Jim and Karen Shepard, Julia Slavin, Flavio Stigliano, Syd Straw, and Abigail Thomas.

Gordon Lish has my gratitude always.

Beloved Robert Jones and Lucy Grealy—"Thou art not gone being gone."

ABOUT THE AUTHOR

AMY HEMPEL is the author of *Tumble Home, At the Gates of the Animal Kingdom,* and *Reasons to Live,* and the coeditor of *Unleashed.* Her stories have appeared in *Elle, GQ, Harper's, Playboy, The Quarterly,* and *Vanity Fair.* She teaches in the Graduate Writing Program at Bennington College and lives in New York City.

"Beach Town" was previously published in *Tin House* and appeared
in *Bestial Noise* (an anthology published by Tin House).
"The Uninvited" was previously published in *GQ*.
"Reference #388475848-5" appeared in *Ontario Review*.
"What Were the White Things?" appeared in *Bellevue Literary Review*.
"The Dog of the Marriage, Part 1" was published as "Now I Can See the Moon"
in *Elle* and reprinted in *Labor Days*.
The *Mississippi Review* first published "The Dog of the Marriage, Part 4."
"The Afterlife" was previously published in *Playboy*.
"Matinee"—now part of "Offertory"—appeared in *Fence*.